Winner of the Prix Littéraire Domitys
Winner of Le Prix des Lecteurs du Livre de Poche

'I'm in story heaven with this book.'

Cecelia Ahern, author of *PS, I Love You*

'Charmingly written, the plot is a continual surprise... Uplifting.'   ***Independent***

'Simply delicious.'   ***Guardian***

'Enthralling... This is that rare book that leaves readers truly humbled, reminding us of everything we should be thankful for, and that it is never too late to do something with our lives.'   ***Bookbag***

'*Sweet Bean Paste* is a sensuous novel, delicately seasoned with mouth-watering culinary magic, to be savoured slowly. A poetic fable on the power of friendship, infused with the genius of simplicity, it will warm even the melancholiest of hearts. In prose tender and lyrical, Sukegawa breathes life into his poignant story, teaching us that no existence is devoid of meaning, and that even the humblest of beings makes a valuable contribution to the world.'

Denis Thériault, author of
The Peculiar Life of a Lonely Postman

'A perfect example of cover & content in total harmony – I love this little masterpiece.'   **Foyles Bookshop**

'A beautifully rendered tale of outsiders coming together.'

B&N Reads

'Sukegawa – enabled by Watts's lucid translation – tells an endearing, thoughtful tale about relationships and the everyday meaning of life… Readers in search of gently illuminating fare – e.g. Shion Miura's *The Great Passage*, Jeff Talarigo's *The Pearl Diver* – will appreciate this toothsome treat.'

Library Journal

'As wise as it is moving, Sukegawa's novel beguiles and seduces the reader from evocative opening to compassionate close.' **Herald, Scotland**

'A tale that's both charming and uplifting.' **Scotsman**

'Although Tokue's past is a reflection of a dark chapter of Japanese history, her wisdom, patience, and kindness shape this touching and occasionally wistful novel. Through Tokue's story, Sukegawa eloquently explores the seeds of biases and challenges us to truly listen to the natural world and the messages it artfully hides.' **Booklist**

'*Sweet Bean Paste* is a subtle, moving exploration of redemption in an unforgiving society… A book with deceptive heft and lingering resonance.' **Japan Times**

'A moving story of dark secrets and the power of friendship.' **Ozy.com**

'*Sweet Bean Paste* is a book for your heart, mind…and appetite… It feels important, significant and far-reaching. It really is a moving and inspiring story which is as heartwarming as a delicious dorayaki, well maybe with a bit of salt. It is not often that a book touches your very soul and, therefore, *Sweet Bean Paste* deserves the highest of marks.'

Thoughts on Papyrus

Sweet Bean Paste

Durian Sukegawa

Translated by Alison Watts

ONEWORLD

A Oneworld Book

First published in North America, Great Britain and Australia
by Oneworld Publications, 2017
Reprinted 2017, 2018 (twice), 2020 and 2021 (three times)
2022 (twice), 2023 (three times) and 2024

Originally published in Japanese as *An*

ISBN 978-1-78607-195-8
eBook ISBN 978-1-78607-196-5

This book is partially funded by a grant from Books from Japan, from the
Japanese Literature Publishing and Promotion Centre

Printed and bound in Great Britain by Clays Ltd, Elcograf S.p.A.

Oneworld Publications
10 Bloomsbury Street
London WC1B 3SR
England

Stay up to date with the latest books,
special offers, and exclusive content from
Oneworld with our newsletter

Sign up on our website
oneworld-publications.com

Sweet
Bean
Paste

I

A sweetly scented breeze blew along Cherry Blossom Street.

Sentaro stood over a hot griddle inside the Doraharu shop, as he did all day everyday, cooking pancakes for his dorayaki. Cherry Blossom Street was a run-down commercial strip in a depressed part of town, a street more notable for empty shops than the cherry trees planted sparsely on either side. Today, however, perhaps because the flowers were in full bloom, there were more people about than usual.

Sentaro looked up to see an elderly lady in a white hat standing on the roadside, but immediately turned back to the bowl of batter he was mixing. He assumed she was looking at the billowing cloud of cherry blossom on the tree outside the shop. When he next looked up, however, she was still there. And it wasn't the flowers, but rather Sentaro himself that she seemed to be observing. He nodded automatically in greeting. The woman smiled stiffly and shuffled closer.

Sentaro recognized her face. She had been at the shop a few days earlier.

'About this,' she said, raising her hand with a slow,

deliberate motion to point at a Help Wanted notice taped to the window. 'Do you *really* mean "age is no object"?'

Sentaro paused in his work. He noticed that her fingers were bent like hooks. 'Got someone in mind? A grandchild, perhaps?'

The woman blinked one eye. A gentle gust of wind shook the tree, setting adrift petals that wafted through the open window to land on the griddle. 'Um...' She leaned forward, 'I wonder if I could apply?'

'Pardon?'

She pointed to herself. 'Can I apply? I always wanted a job like this.'

Sentaro laughed before he could stop himself. 'May I ask how old you are?'

'I'm seventy-six.'

How could he send her away without causing offence? Sentaro scraped the spatula on the edge of the bowl while he groped for the right words.

'Well, the pay's not much. I can only manage six hundred yen an hour.'

'Sorry? What's that?' The woman cupped her hand around her ear.

Sentaro leaned over, the way he did when he handed dorayaki to children and elderly customers.

'I said the pay's not much. I appreciate the offer, but I'm not sure. At your age...'

'Oh, you mean the pay.' She ran her bent fingers over the words on the notice. 'I'll do it for half that. Three hundred yen.'

'Three hundred yen?'

The woman's eyes crinkled in a smile beneath the brim of her hat.

'Ah, I think...No, I'm afraid it won't work. I hope you understand.'

'My name's Tokue Yoshii.'

'Sorry?' Sentaro realized that she must be hard of hearing and misunderstood. He shook his head to signal his meaning. 'I do apologize.'

'Oh?' Tokue Yoshii stared at Sentaro. He noticed that her eyes were different shapes, and one side of her face appeared stiff.

'It's heavy work, you know. It'd be a bit...'

Tokue opened her mouth as if to take a deep breath, then suddenly pointed behind her. 'Who planted this cherry tree?'

'Pardon?'

'The cherry tree,' she repeated, turning her face toward the blossoms. 'Who planted it?'

Sentaro looked up at the flowers, now at their peak. 'What do you mean, who?'

'*Somebody* must've planted it.'

'Sorry, don't know. I don't come from round here.'

Unspoken thoughts flitted across Tokue's face, but seeing Sentaro pick up the rubber spatula, she simply said, 'I'll see you again,' and backed away from the window. She walked off in the opposite direction from the train station with an awkward, stiff gait. Sentaro looked down and went back to his mixing.

3

2

Doraharu opened for business seven days a week, all year round. Every morning, come eleven o'clock, Sentaro would raise the shutters for the day. He usually donned his cook's clothes just two hours before opening time to begin preparing the pancake batter and sweet bean paste for making dorayaki. Most confectioners spent longer than that, but things were done differently at Doraharu.

Today, like any other day, Sentaro drank his regular morning can of coffee and then proceeded to kick-push a cardboard box into the kitchen from the pavement outside. It contained a delivery of Chinese-made *tsubuan*, the coarse sweet bean paste that he used for his dorayaki filling. His late boss had always used readymade bean paste and Sentaro simply continued the practice. A friendly wholesaler regularly delivered five-kilogram boxes of it.

Sentaro took a plastic tub from inside, and set about mixing the contents with leftover bean paste from the day before. Operations at Doraharu relied heavily on the fact that bean paste could be refrigerated for short periods without too much loss of aroma or quality.

Although it was not illegal to recycle the filling in this fashion, this was not exactly standard procedure with most confectioners.

But that was how things were done at Doraharu, a business that did just enough trade to stay afloat. Sentaro never sold enough to use up a whole container of bean paste in one day; there were always leftovers. Every morning he combined the previous day's leftover bean paste with a new batch so that eventually it all got used up.

Once the bean paste was ready Sentaro began preparing the batter. This was also available for supply by wholesalers, but it was expensive, and so he preferred to make it himself. He heaped the ingredients in a bowl, mixed them together, and turned on the gas to heat the flat griddle. When the temperature was right he carefully ladled spoonfuls of batter onto the hot surface with the gong-shaped spoon from which dorayaki took their name: *dora* for gong, and *yaki* for grilled. Once the small, fluffy pancakes were ready he arranged them in rows in a heated glass case to keep warm. Now it was time to open. Sentaro sighed as he lifted the shutters from inside, a blank expression on his face.

Lunchtime came and Sentaro was sitting in the shop's kitchen picking at a lunch from the convenience store when he saw a white hat appear on the other side of the window.

'The old lady,' he muttered.

She was smiling at him, and he felt obliged to stand up. 'Err, hello again.'

'Hello.'

'Can I do something for you?'

Tokue pulled a piece of paper from her handbag. 'This is how I write my name.'

'Huh?' Sentaro glanced at the paper. Her name was written in blue ink, in a distinctive style with every stroke formed by a curling flourish. 'Sorry,' he said, 'but you still can't work here.' He pushed the paper back to her.

Tokue went to pick it up with her bent fingers, but then seemed to change her mind and gently withdrew her hand. 'As you can see, I have a bit of trouble with my fingers, so I don't mind working for less than I said last time. Two hundred yen will do.'

'For what?'

'My hourly pay.'

'That's not the issue.'

Sentaro repeated what he'd said before about not being able to hire her. Tokue's reaction was to simply stare back at him, like last time. Sentaro stepped away from the counter and reached into the warmer to take out a dorayaki. He thought that if he gave her one maybe she would go away.

'Do you make the bean paste yourself?' Tokue suddenly asked, as if she'd read his mind.

'Ah, that's um, a trade secret.' Sentaro replied, his Adam's apple bobbing nervously.

Had she seen something? He looked over his shoulder to check. The tub of sweet bean paste was sitting in plain view on the kitchen bench next to his lunch, with the lid off and a spoon sticking out to boot. Sentaro shuffled sideways to block Tokue's view.

'I had one of your dorayaki the other day. The pancake wasn't too bad, I thought, but the bean paste, well...'

'The bean paste?'

'Yes. I couldn't tell anything about the feelings of the person who made it.'

'You couldn't? That's strange.' Sentaro made a face as if to show how regrettable that was, though he knew full well his bean paste could reveal no such thing.

'It was sort of...lacking.'

'Bean paste is very difficult, you know. Listen, lady— err, Ma'am. Have you ever made it?'

'I certainly have. I've been making it for fifty years.'

Sentaro almost dropped the dorayaki he was about to put in a paper bag. 'Fifty years?'

'Yes, half a century. Bean paste is all about feeling, young man.'

'Oh. Feeling, eh,' Sentaro said as he pushed the dorayaki package toward Tokue. For one fleeting moment he felt buffeted, as if by a sudden gust of wind.

'But...' He hesitated. 'Sorry. I still can't hire you.'

'Really?'

'I'm sorry. That's how it is.'

Tokue stared at him with her mismatched eyes, then pulled a cloth purse from her handbag.

7

'That's okay,' he said. 'It's on the house.'

'Why? It costs 140 yen, doesn't it?' She fumbled about in her purse to extract the coins. It took some time for her to find a 100-yen coin and four 10-yen coins, then line them up on the narrow counter beneath the window. Every finger was slightly crooked and her thumb was bent backwards. 'Young man...'

'What?'

Tokue rummaged in her bag again. 'Try some of this,' she said, pulling out a round Tupperware container in a plastic bag. Sentaro could see through the bag that it contained a dark substance.

'What is it?' As Sentaro picked up the container, Tokue began edging away from the counter. 'Is this bean paste?'

But she was already gone, and only turned back to give a quick nod before disappearing around the corner.

3

That night, Sentaro went out for a drink. He chose a noodle restaurant in the downtown area, where he ordered warmed sake accompanied by a small side-dish of tempura and soba noodles in hot broth. Over sips of sake interspersed with mouthfuls of food, he thought about the day's events.

After Tokue's departure, Sentaro had tossed the Tupperware container straight into the rubbish bin. It wasn't as if he didn't feel bad about doing this, he just didn't want to get in any deeper. Every time he lifted the bin lid, however, it met his eyes, until eventually he was moved to fish it out. He intended to have a small taste – just a mouthful – to satisfy his conscience and be done with it. But that one mouthful brought an exclamation of astonishment to his lips.

Tokue's bean paste was like nothing he had ever tasted before. It had a rich aroma, and sweetness that spread across his palette. The substance he bought in plastic containers could not compare.

'Fifty years, eh?' he mused, lifting the sake cup to his lips again and recalling the taste which had so unexpectedly rooted him to the spot. 'She's been making it longer than I've been alive.'

He looked at the restaurant menu tacked to the wall. The noodle chef had handwritten it himself with a brush, and whenever Sentaro saw that careful calligraphy it always reminded him of his mother.

'That old lady'd be about the same age as Mum.' In his mind he saw his mother's small frame seated at a low floor table, her shoulders rounded as she bent over, writing deftly on the stationery spread out before her.

Sentaro tended to cut his memories short at this point. Usually he tried not to think about his long-dead mother and the father he'd not seen in a decade. Tonight, however, he couldn't manage to keep the memories at bay. An image of the mother who had taught him to read and write as a small boy refused to leave his mind.

'Oh, hell.' Sentaro expelled a stream of sake-laden breath. By the time he was out from behind bars his mother was no longer in this world.

You never knew what the future held, he mused. Look at the path he'd ended up on, instead of becoming a writer as he hoped. And how he had passed the days these last few years, standing in front of a griddle cooking dorayaki. Never once had he imagined himself doing that.

Sentaro filled his cup with more sake and gulped down the strong alcohol without pause, as if to wash away a bitterness that had built up in his mouth.

Memories of his mother...She was softly spoken but troubled by anxieties beneath the surface that she could not conceal. Then there were the loud disputes with his father, and arguments with relatives that made her cry and scream. As a child Sentaro had been frightened by these outbursts, that's why he'd wished there could always be cake on the table. Because his mother had a sweet tooth, and whenever they had the sweet things that she liked, such as *manju* buns or cake, she would be in a good mood and he could also feel at peace. He loved his mother when she smiled and said to him, 'Mm, isn't this delicious, Sen?'

Again he thought of Tokue Yoshii's remarkable bean paste. He tried to imagine his mother's expression if she had still been alive to taste it. What would she have said?

This thought led to another. Maybe there were people who would be pleased by it. And, he added to himself, it would only cost 200 yen an hour. Was the old lady really serious? If that was all she wanted, maybe he could have her help out.

Sentaro considered the possibility.

He didn't have that notice in the window because business was so busy he needed help. He simply wanted somebody around for company. Dorayaki weren't much as conversation partners.

Would the old lady really take two hundred yen?

He did the calculations in his drink-fuddled head. If he paid Tokue Yoshii the amount she proposed, it'd be as good as free labour. On top of which he'd get that amazing sweet bean paste thrown in! Then if sales went up as a result, he might be able to increase his monthly debt repayments, and that would mean he could move forward his day of release from this toil.

But – and here Sentaro's hand holding the sake cup wavered in mid-air – he couldn't help feeling uncomfortable about her fingers. He saw them in his mind. No doubt customers would balk too if they noticed them.

Another idea flashed into his head: he could get her to just make the sweet bean paste. Sentaro nodded to himself. Yes, that was it – she could just stay in the kitchen and make the bean paste. While she was doing that he might be able to get the secret of making it from her. At that age she'd probably get tired and quit soon anyway.

'That's right, customers don't have to see her,' he muttered aloud.

The proprietor, who was talking with a patron at another table, looked over at him. He narrowed his eyes in inquiry at Sentaro. Sentaro shrugged and lifted his sake bottle in reply.

'Another one,' he said.

4

A few days later, Sentaro looked up from the griddle to see the elderly lady in the white hat standing under the cherry tree again. She was looking at him with a smile.

'Hello.' Sentaro spoke first.

Tokue's smile widened to reveal her teeth. She walked towards him with swaying, clumsy steps.

'The petals have all fallen now, haven't they?'

'Yes, sure have.' Sentaro looked up at the tree too.

'Now is a good time for leaf-viewing.'

'Leaf-viewing?'

'Yes, when the leaves are at their best. Look, up there.'

Sentaro looked in the direction Tokue pointed and saw buds of new foliage in the swaying treetops.

'See, they're waving their hands at you.'

When you put it like that, there was some resemblance, he thought. The overlapping leaves moving to and fro did look a bit like children holding hands and swinging them. He mumbled something in agreement and turned to Tokue again.

'Um, I want to say...'

'Yes?'

'That bean paste you gave me was delicious.'

'Ah, so you tried it.'

'Yes. And I wondered if you'd like to come and help out here.'

Tokue looked puzzled. 'What?'

'Could you make that bean paste for me here?'

Tokue looked at Sentaro with her mouth hanging half-open. 'Yes...Really?'

'Only make the bean paste, mind you. I don't need help with customers.'

'Oh?'

An awkward silence ensued as Tokue continued staring at Sentaro. He beckoned for her to come in and take a seat at the inside counter. She entered, sat down on a chair, and took off her hat. Her scalp was visible under white hair.

'Can you manage lifting the cooking pans? They're quite heavy. You need to be strong to make bean paste.'

'You could lift the pans for me.'

'Yes, I suppose so,' said Sentaro distractedly, looking at Tokue's hands. She had them clasped in such a way as to hide the gnarled fingers. 'Can you hold a wooden spoon all right?'

'Yes.'

'Excuse me for asking, but what happened to your hands?'

'Ah, my hands.'

Sentaro noticed they were tightly gripped.

'I had an illness when I was young and this is a

side-effect. I know they don't look so good but I don't think it'll be a problem.'

'Well, that's why all I'm asking is for you to make bean paste. That's enough.'

'But I really can work here, can't I?' Tokue looked at him and smiled. The movement caused the skin on her right cheek to stretch taut, as if there was a hard board concealed underneath. Sentaro wondered if that was what made her eyes appear to be different shapes.

'Yes, you can. What should I call you? Mrs... Miss...'

'Tokue is fine. And what's your name, young man?'

'Sentaro Tsujii.'

'Sentaro Tsujii? What a lovely name. It sounds like an actor.'

'Hah, I don't think so. It's just me...'

At Tokue's request Sentaro wrote down the characters for his name on a scrap of paper.

'And what should I call you?'

'Sentaro will do.'

'In that case, Sentaro. Do you make the bean paste here?'

'Err...well—' Sentaro was suddenly stuck for words. He didn't know what to say. 'Ah, to tell the truth, it doesn't turn out even when I do make it myself. Sometimes it smells burnt.'

'Hmm, yes I see,' said Tokue, eyeing the pots and cooker with an expression that said she could well understand why.

Sentaro stood up to serve tea, blocking her gaze at the same time.

'Where've you been making it for fifty years? At a confectioner's shop?'

'I, err...'

'At home?'

Sentaro didn't really care where she made it. He didn't care who she was, either. All that concerned him was if she could make a good-quality, sweet bean paste to draw in the customers and help get him away from this shop as soon as possible.

'Oh, a lot of things happened—it's a long story,' she said.

It was clear to Sentaro that Tokue was not being entirely straight with him, but then he didn't want to be quizzed about his own past, either. 'Really, well, I suppose so,' he replied.

'Do you own this shop, Sentaro?'

'No, it's more like the extension of a casual job.'

'So there's someone else. The owner?'

'My former boss used to run the shop and work here. Now his wife owns it.'

'So you're not really responsible.'

'Not exactly that either.'

'Should I introduce myself to her?'

'She's not in good health at the moment and sometimes can't even come by once a week. Another time.'

Sentaro thought he detected an expression of relief pass over Tokue's face when she heard that.

'What about your boss?'

'He passed away.'

'Oh, I see.'

Sentaro took advantage of the pause in conversation to push a notebook and pen over to Tokue. 'Okay, lady— err...Tokue, can you write your full name and contact details for me, please?'

Tokue looked at the paper with a strained expression. 'My fingers...' she said hesitatingly.

Here we go already, Sentaro thought, wanting to look the other way. But after a brief interval Tokue picked up the pen and wrote her name, carefully forming each character stroke by stroke, in the same quirky, distinctive handwriting that Sentaro had previously seen. It took some time for her to complete the task. The writing made a bold impression, penned with such force it left imprints several pages deep.

'What about a phone number? For emergency contact. Don't you have a mobile phone?'

'I don't have a telephone. The post will do.'

'That's not what I meant...'

'It's all right. I won't be late. I'm up before the birds.'

'But it's not...'

Looking at the address, Sentaro saw she had written the name of a district that was on the outskirts of the city. He had an odd feeling it should mean something to him, but couldn't say why.

5

The second hand moved around the clock.

Sentaro lay with his hands on the quilt, staring up at the dark ceiling. The whisky he'd drunk as a nightcap had not helped him fall asleep.

He twisted his head to reach out for the clock next to the pillow and brushed the alarm button with his fingers to check that it was set. Tokue Yoshii was going to come once every two days to make coarse sweet bean paste for him, starting tomorrow morning. He couldn't very well be late. That's why he'd gone to bed earlier than usual.

Who was that old lady?

Even though he'd made it clear she was coming only to make bean paste, Sentaro still felt uneasy. Tokue sometimes said things that seemed off the mark. Although her deafness could account for it, Sentaro did not think that was the reason. It was not as if she didn't have her wits about her, and although she smiled mildly enough, he had observed a determined gleam in the back of her eyes. Not to mention the challenging looks she threw him at times.

After Tokue had written her address Sentaro had

revealed how the shop was run. He told her about always buying wholesale bean paste and only beginning preparations two hours before opening.

'Why?' she had asked loudly. 'If you want to use freshly made bean paste you need to start before the sun is up.'

'But I can get bean paste brought here with just one phone call.'

'What are you saying?! Bean paste is the soul of dorayaki, boss!'

'Yeah...that's why I asked you to work here.'

'If you were a customer, would you line up for dorayaki from this shop?'

'Now, look here...well, maybe not.'

She had given him quite a talking-to. He might be the one in charge, but he could hardly answer back. In the end he agreed to comply with her instructions: they were to begin preparing at six in the morning. Sentaro was to be in the kitchen before then to start boiling the adzuki beans, and Tokue would catch the first bus in order to arrive soon after. He sighed at the thought; this was turning out to be a hassle.

Sentaro was in his fourth year at Doraharu. He worked hard, with no regular day off, but never once had he risen that early to get to work.

Why had he taken the old lady on, he wondered ruefully. Had he made a bad decision? This was not what he expected. She was more demanding than first impressions suggested.

'What've I done...?' He was fed up before they'd even started.

There was also another reason for his sighs. How was he going to tell the shop owner? That was going to be a problem.

The owner was the wife of Sentaro's former boss, and since the death of her husband she had developed all kinds of health problems. She did not care to eat dorayaki any more because of the sugar content. Whenever she came to check the books or for some other reason her expression was unfriendly, and though she had always been slightly neurotic, now she was fussier than ever about hygiene. Sentaro had been scolded any number of times about his cleaning methods.

Once he had taken on a student part-time without consulting her. She had been continually sarcastic about the boy, but when someone reported to her that he was smoking behind the shop, she became livid. Sentaro had received a phone call from her, of course. She'd immediately begun haranguing him about what would happen if the shop started to smell. Next time he wanted to hire somebody, she warned, she would have to be present at the interview.

Maybe he should keep quiet about Tokue Yoshii for a while. As he tossed and turned, Sentaro decided to do just that. He didn't even know yet whether she could actually work with those crippled fingers of hers.

He rolled onto his back and clicked his tongue in irritation. Now it was the faces of the school girls who hung around his shop that he saw. They always came in a group, occupied the only five seats at the counter, made a lot of noise, and left food scattered about when they left. Just the other day they'd complained about cherry-blossom petals in the dorayaki. Sentaro usually kept the window open, and during cherry-blossom season petals sometimes drifted in, falling into the pancakes as they cooked. Sentaro had apologized when this happened and offered the girl another dorayaki. But that only set the others off. They wouldn't keep quiet about it and teasingly complained about petals in their own dorayaki. Then one got out her phone and started broadcasting to all her friends that there was free dorayaki.

What would those kids say if they saw the old lady's fingers? And what would she say in turn about their outrageous behaviour?

It was all too much, Sentaro thought. He couldn't stop tossing and turning.

'Those monkeys, what were they thinking?... Cherry-blossom petals, my foot.'

Sentaro batted the quilt with his hands, and then reached for the alarm clock once more.

6

In the morning Tokue Yoshii was already waiting beneath the cherry tree when Sentaro arrived, slightly late.

'There're some small cherries,' she said in reply to Sentaro's apology, pointing to the treetop above her.

'Did you manage to get a bus?' he asked, for he was sure there could not be any buses running at this time of day.

'Oh, never mind about that,' she said and headed for the back door, dodging the question.

In the kitchen the bowl of adzuki beans that Sentaro had left to soak overnight was waiting on the bench. The beans had swelled to fill the bowl. Every bean sparkled, transforming the atmosphere of the kitchen. Sentaro felt as if he were looking at a living creature rather than food.

'Mm, lovely,' said Tokue, bringing her face up close to the bowl.

The adzuki were not from Obihiro or Tamba, or any other area known for quality beans. Average customer-spend at Doraharu put those more expensive adzuki beans out of reach for Sentaro. When he explained that to Tokue, she said that she was happy to try beans from elsewhere. It was a nuisance, but Sentaro contacted a dealer and arranged for a delivery of Canadian beans to start with.

Sentaro had done the calculations. He estimated that they could use two kilograms of raw beans per batch of bean paste. Soaking the beans overnight would more than double their weight, bringing it to a good four kilograms. After boiling they would simmer in a syrup of granulated sugar, with the amount of sugar to be added calculated at 70 per cent of the weight after soaking. That would bring the total weight of the bean paste to just below seven kilograms. Assuming twenty grams of bean paste for each dorayaki, albeit measured by eye, he estimated that they could make between 330 and 340 dorayaki with each batch. This should last for several days at current rates of consumption, since he never got through all of a five-kilogram batch of the readymade bean paste in one day.

'Before boiling...' Tokue muttered, carefully examining every bean one by one. 'Sentaro, did you take a good look at the beans before you put them in to soak?

'Look at what?'

'The beans.'

Sentaro shook his head.

'I thought so. Not all these beans are suitable.'

Tokue scooped some out with her bent fingers. She picked out several and spread them out on her palm to show Sentaro. The skin was still hard on some, while others had burst or split.

'You have to check. If they've already split it can affect quality. Beans from overseas aren't always selected carefully.'

Sentaro thought her handling of the beans was odd. The way she brought her face up close to them, so close it was almost as if she were communicating with them. Even after they had been put into the copper pot to cook, her attitude did not change.

On the occasions when Sentaro had attempted to make bean paste, he always left the beans on the stove to cook until they were soft. Not Tokue, however; her method was completely different.

To begin with, she immediately added more water as soon as the water was about to boil. She did this several times, then drained the beans in a strainer and threw away the cooking water. After that she returned them to the pot to soak in fresh lukewarm water; that would remove the bitterness and astringency, she said. Next she stirred them gently with a wooden spatula, taking care not to squash them while letting them simmer thoroughly over a low heat. At every stage in this process Tokue kept her face so close to the beans it was enveloped in steam. What was she looking at, Sentaro wondered. Was she watching for some kind of change? He moved closer to examine the adzuki through the haze of steam but couldn't see anything significant.

He watched Tokue holding the wooden spoon with her gammy hands as she scrutinized the beans, observing her side-on. Sentaro hoped that she wasn't going to require the same level of enthusiasm from him. Just the thought of it made his spirits sink.

Without quite knowing why, however, Sentaro found himself also drawn to gazing at the beans in the pot. He watched them jiggle about, covered by the water; not a single one lost its shape.

When there was just a little cooking water left in the pot, Tokue turned off the flame and placed a chopping board on top as a lid. This would steam them she told Sentaro. All these steps were completely new to him.

'It's all very complicated,' he blurted out.

'It's just good hospitality,' Tokue countered.

'For the customers?'

'No. The beans.'

'The beans?'

'Because they came all the way from Canada. For us.'

After a few minutes Tokue removed the chopping board. She stared at the adzuki while pouring cold water into the copper pot. They were now at the soaking stage, she told Sentaro. This involved immersing the beans in water, letting them soak for a while, then discarding that water and pouring fresh water in. The process was repeated until the water ran clear. Tokue stared at the beans as she poured. She kept her face up close, stroking them with her fingertips. It looked to Sentaro like she was panning for gold.

'Nobody's ever worked as hard in this shop before.'

'You have to do it properly or else all the trouble you've gone to this far will be wasted.'

Sentaro could only stare at her, his arms folded across his chest.

'I was wondering – why do you look at them like that?'

'Eh?'

'What are you looking for when you put your face so close to the beans?'

'I just do all I can for them.'

'All you can?'

'All right, boss, lift this pot for me, please?'

Sentaro changed places with Tokue and lifted it with both hands. He poured it over the strainer in the sink and the water drained away, revealing the cooked beans.

'Oh...they're beautiful.'

Sentaro leaned over for a closer look. These were a far cry from his own attempts; he had to admit that the skill with which they'd been cooked was obvious. Despite all the simmering, every single bean still looked firm and taut, with no wrinkles. Whenever Sentaro had tried to make bean paste, most of the beans were usually split by this stage, with the starch spilling out from their insides. These beans, on the other hand, simply shone – each one in perfect, sparkling order.

'I didn't know they could cook up like this.' Sentaro gazed admiringly.

Tokue shrugged her shoulders and smiled. 'Cook up? Have you ever really made bean paste before, boss?'

'Ah, well, I tried...but, you know.'

'Well, you'll have to do some study then.'

Sentaro did the rest of the work after that. The next task was to make the syrup for sweetening the raw bean paste. He poured two litres of water into the now empty pot and brought it to the boil. To that he added two and a half kilograms of granulated sugar and dissolved it.

Tokue stood at his side, explaining the vital points.

He continued to stir the syrup slowly, even after the granules of sugar had dissolved, so that it would not boil more than necessary. Next he carefully added the prepared beans, paying close attention to the level of heat. Then it was time to blend the beans and syrup.

'This is crucial,' Tokue told him, 'because it burns easily. So make sure to keep the tip of the wooden spatula against the bottom of the pan as you stir.'

This, too, was new to Sentaro. He did as he was told, while Tokue added salt to the pot. She reeled off a stream of detailed instructions:

'If you burn it now it's ruined.'

'Keep the spatula upright.'

'Make it speedy.'

'Don't rush.'

27

A surprising amount of sweat poured from Sentaro's brow and the back of his neck as he stood over the hot mixture.

Nevertheless, he realized that Tokue was indeed right. Whenever Sentaro had tried to make bean paste, this was the point at which he always failed. Once blended with the sugar, the bean paste tended to burn easily on the bottom, but if he tried to avoid this by turning the flame low, it took longer and the quality suffered proportionately. In order to make bean paste that had a pleasing texture in the mouth and still looked good to the eye, it was necessary to maintain a certain temperature to reduce the moisture. But to do this without burning, he was discovering, you had to make bold movements with the wooden spatula at the right time.

Sentaro wiped the sweat from his brow with the sleeve of his shirt while manipulating the spatula. And then, when he least expected it, 'That's enough now. Turn the gas off,' Tokue instructed.

'But it's still runny.'

'It's just right. Timing's important here.'

'Hang on...This—'

The substance in the copper pot was still too soft to be called bean paste. Sentaro might not be skilled at making sweet bean paste, but he knew what consistency it should be for making dorayaki. If he tried to sandwich this between the pancakes it would just run out the sides. He did as Tokue instructed though, and kept stirring with the spatula after the heat was turned off. As he did so, the runny paste gradually began to take on the right quality. Tokue spread a cloth over the chopping board.

'Now we leave it for a while to steep in the syrup. After that we'll scoop it out with a spatula and spread it on here.'

'What?'

'The paste you just blended.'

Sentaro looked confused.

Tokue took the spatula from him. 'Let's have a little rest, shall we, boss?'

7

Tokue told Sentaro to write down all the steps they had just covered while the paste was steeping in the syrup.

'I can remember from watching,' he answered.

But when she challenged him to tell her from the beginning, he reluctantly pulled out a notebook.

'You're full of confidence, aren't you?' she said.

'No, not really.'

'Why don't you take notes then? It's the fine points that matter with confectionery. How can you remember anything if you don't write it down?'

'Err...'

Abashed, Sentaro made notes as Tokue explained it all again, starting with the soaking stage.

'Where did you learn to do this?' he asked.

'It's only because I've been doing it so long.'

'Fifty years, right?'

'You must get a lot of customers my age.'

Sentaro shook his head.

'The school girls are pretty rowdy. I sometimes get fed up with their noise.'

A faint flush entered Tokue's cheeks. 'Ah...Girls

that age,' she said, 'it's only natural they get excited. They could be doing worse things.'

'I only put up with it because they're customers.'

'I can meet them, can't I?'

Sentaro couldn't bring himself to say no, even though he had not changed his mind about having Tokue leave once they finished making bean paste, specifically so she would not meet the customers. He was determined not to give way on that.

Tokue peered into the pot and stirred the syrup-soaked beans with the wooden spatula. 'It's just right.'

She scooped up some bean paste with the spatula and put it directly on the cotton cloth.

'I didn't know you had to do this, too,' Sentaro observed.

'They're still sweating, so you need to absorb that. By the time it cools you'll have some lovely bean paste.'

Steam rose off the paste in the wake of the spatula moving through it. When spread out on the cotton cloth the paste shone and a deep smooth aroma filled the entire kitchen.

'Now we need to find out if this bean paste will go with your pancakes.'

Sentaro trickled batter from the *dora* spoon over the hot griddle.

Making the pancakes was the only thing his boss had taught him how to do properly. The batter was a

31

standard mixture of eggs, high-quality sugar and soft cake flour combined in equal measures. Sometimes Sentaro added a little baking soda or sweet *mirin* cooking sake, or water to adjust the viscosity, but the basic three-equal-parts recipe never changed throughout the year. It was an instinctive and elegantly simple recipe that anybody could make once they got used to it.

Cooking was the hard part. Unlike other similar traditional sweets made with sweet bean paste, *Imagawayaki* for example, which were cooked in a mould, dorayaki were cooked on a flat griddle, and it was the cook who determined the size and thickness, aiming to produce consistently uniform pancakes by finding the right rhythm and movement. Seasoned cooks always made it look easy, but it was a tricky process for beginners to master. The slightest difference in water-amounts could affect the size, and there was no guarantee that the batter would pour onto the griddle and form a perfect circle in the first place. On top of this, the batter burned very easily if the cook got the timing wrong.

Today, unusually, Sentaro managed to cook all the pancakes to perfection in an evenly round size. Maybe it was the thought of having quality bean paste for the first time, or perhaps it was due to a healthy tension brought about by Tokue's presence.

They had started work sometime after six and had now been toiling for four and a half hours. With fifteen minutes to go until the shop opened, Sentaro and Tokue sat on the kitchen stools, stretching and rubbing their arms.

They sandwiched the still-warm bean paste between the fluffy, freshly grilled pancakes. For anyone who liked dorayaki, this was a moment of happy anticipation. Sentaro gave a nod of thanks in Tokue's direction, and then brought the dorayaki to his lips.

The aroma seemed to leap up at him, as if it were alive, racing through his nose to the back of his head. Unlike the ready-made paste, this was the smell of fresh, living beans. It had depth. It had life. A mellow, sweet taste unfurled inside Sentaro's mouth.

Sentaro was bowled over. He smiled at Tokue and took another bite. Same again. He was knocked out by this flavour. 'Hmm,' he murmured, stroking his cheek. 'This is really something.'

'What do you think, boss?'

'Never tasted bean paste like it.'

'Really?'

'Finally, a sweet bean paste I can eat.'

'What?' Tokue stared at the dorayaki Sentaro held in his hand. Teeth marks were visible. 'What did you say, boss?' Her hand, still holding her own partially eaten dorayaki, was frozen in mid-air.

'Ah, I, err...'

'Yes?' Tokue put her dorayaki down on the plate.

'I almost never eat a whole dorayaki.'

'You what?' Tokue's mouth hung open. 'How can

33

that be? You make them. Don't tell me you don't like them?'

Sentaro hastily shook his head. 'No, that's not it. I do eat them, I just don't have much of a sweet tooth.'

'Well, I never.'

'But I can tell that your bean paste is special. I thought so before, but this...Never had anything like it.'

'Sentaro, let me get this straight. You don't like sweet food?' she said, with her eyes glued to his face.

'It's not that I don't like sweet food, more that I can't eat a whole...err...'

'My goodness, boss.' The more Sentaro's voice trailed away, the louder Tokue's became. 'So why are you working in a dorayaki shop?'

'Well, that's a good question.'

Tokue stared at him incredulously.

'Um, it just came about somehow that I ended up working here.'

'Somehow...?'

'Well, there were...circumstances.' Sentaro picked up his still unfinished dorayaki and took another bite. 'But this...'

'What? You're not one to make yourself clear.'

'I just realized that your bean paste is so good, it makes the pancake seem superfluous. It's unbalanced.'

Tokue turned to take another bite of her dorayaki and put the rest in her mouth. 'Well, now that you mention it.'

'I'm right, aren't I? This bean paste is so good it's all you notice. There's no point using it with these pancakes. If anything, they're in the way.'

Even as he spoke Sentaro heard a voice screaming in his head: Don't make any more work for yourself. But the words were already forming. 'If the pancakes were better, it'd be much better overall, don't you think?'

'Can you improve them any?'

'Maybe. But for now at least we'll have decent bean paste for the first time ever in Doraharu.'

'Praise like that won't change anything. You disappoint me, boss. How can someone who doesn't like sweet food be running a dorayaki shop?'

'I told you that's not what I meant. Look. I ate it all.' Sentaro brushed his empty hands together, wiping off the crumbs to emphasize his point. 'I haven't done that in a long time.'

'Oh, it really is too bad.' Tokue shook her head in disbelief.

'Well, I was more interested in this,' said Sentaro, lifting his hand up in the motion of pouring sake.

Tokue wrinkled up her nose. 'You should be running a bar.'

He had no answer to this, and stood up to open the shutters.

8

The sweet bean paste in Doraharu has changed. Sentaro thought about writing an announcement of some kind to put in the shop window, but decided against it in the end, in case customers wondered about the bean paste he had used up to then.

Nevertheless, Sentaro noticed an immediate change from the day he started making bean paste with Tokue. The usually noisy crowd of school girls were strangely quiet.

'This tastes better, somehow,' one observed, looking at Sentaro.

Sentaro shrugged this aside with a vague reply about good beans, and didn't mention Tokue.

Customers who bought takeaway also commented. 'Have you got a new supplier?' one said.

When Tokue came next, Sentaro reported this to her. 'That's nice,' she said with a smile, without a word of self-praise for her own role.

'But sales haven't improved. If people are going to say good things they could at least buy more,' Sentaro complained.

'We should simply be grateful they come at all.'

'But you don't get bean paste like this so easily.'

'Yes, but the world isn't an easy place...'

'Yeah, well, I guess so.'

Sentaro held the wooden spatula in his hand while Tokue stood at his side gazing intently at the beans in the bowl, as always.

Tokue consistently turned out excellent bean paste; she never had a bad day. Sentaro had the feeling that it was her posture while she worked that ensured this. She treated the adzuki beans with the greatest of care, always bringing her face up close to them, painstakingly carrying out every step in the process of cooking, and moving her fingers as if there were nothing wrong with them.

When Tokue said she wanted to try beans from other sources, Sentaro got the supplier to deliver Chinese beans from Shandong Province and US beans as well. Both cooked up well in Tokue's hands; each emitted a deep yet slightly different aroma, and both shone in distinctively different ways. 'Interesting,' she pronounced.

Using different beans made the cooking procedure just that little bit more complicated. Sentaro could see that it meant more work ahead, but by now he too had become mesmerized by the whole process. He briefly considered other ideas, like selling dorayaki according to the beans' place of origin, since it seemed to make such a difference. Or making more money by branching out into other types of Japanese confectionery for which bean paste was the main or only ingredient, such as adzuki bean jelly or *kintsuba*. The bottom line, however, was that he did not want to make any more work for himself.

Sentaro threw himself doggedly into the unfamiliar work of making bean paste. It was a testing time. Physically tiring, of course, but in addition to that Sentaro was annoyed with himself, he couldn't quite believe he was actually doing this, considering what his intentions had been all along. But he began to sense that if he applied himself seriously now, adzuki beans might just open a door for him. While one part of him relished the novel sensation, another part was wary. Whatever happened, though, unless he bid farewell to this life constantly chained to the grill, he could not devote his days to writing again. That much was certain.

Whether it was because of these conflicted feelings, or because he was fundamentally not suited for this work, Sentaro was a long way off being able to make consistently good-quality bean paste on the days when Tokue was not there. Just as he thought he had improved, the next batch would scorch, or the beans become sticky and gluey from over-stirring, or dried out from over-evaporation.

Since he had decided not to use commercial bean paste any more, Sentaro had no choice but to mix his own in with Tokue's when it looked like running out.

Whenever Tokue tasted this mixture he felt like a kid back at school again, waiting to receive his test results. She would sit straight-backed and bring a spoonful of the bean paste to her mouth. Then, staring into space, she would say something like, 'The flavour is struggling a little,' and move her eyes. That didn't mean she was rejecting it, however, for she would always add some comment such as, 'But it's interesting.' Tokue was a stickler in the extreme during the process of making the bean paste, but when it came to tasting the results, the opposite if anything was true; she actually seemed to enjoy a variation in quality.

'I thought I'd have to start over.'

'But this is better than the bought stuff,' she commented.

'Surprisingly.'

'The beans did their best.'

Once her work was over and Tokue relaxed, her language and outlook became more upbeat. While Sentaro was grateful for this, at the same time it sowed the seeds of trouble for him.

No matter how much he told Tokue that she shouldn't show herself to the customers, she would always stay in the kitchen for an hour or two after Doraharu opened, and Sentaro weakened. Because of course she had good reason. She was old. And her body was infirm. Over time she came to occupy the chair in the kitchen for a long while after finishing her work. 'I'm tired,' she would say, or 'My back...'

and sit there frozen with the apron on her knees, her mouth hanging open and a blank look on her face. At times like this she seemed too weak even to drink tea. Whenever there was an announcement outside on the public loudspeaker, she would say, 'What was that?' since she was hard of hearing at the best of times, and look at Sentaro in inquiry. He could hardly say 'Go home now,' even though he wanted to, and so often she was still there when customers began arriving. This is not good, Sentaro always thought.

Tokue at least made a show of trying to stay out of sight, even if she made no move to leave, but if a customer holding a baby happened to appear in front of the window, she would lean out of the shadows, half-showing her face, and cluck, 'Oh, my, my, my.' When groups of children appeared, she would say within earshot, 'Give them a little extra, boss, go on.' It was only then that Sentaro would be driven to say loudly, in spite of himself, 'Isn't it time for you to be leaving?' Upon which Tokue would open the back door and quietly disappear.

The days became warmer and before long it was midsummer. One afternoon, Sentaro opened the door of the refrigerator and let out a small groan. Though the customers were not exactly forming a queue, there had been an unending stream and Sentaro had gone to replenish the bean paste from the refrigerator, because he was on the verge of running out, only to find there was none left. Unless he made another batch, he couldn't serve any more customers. To run out of bean paste, during daylight hours at that, was a first for Sentaro.

After apologizing to the waiting customers he went to find the 'Sold Out' sign to hang in the window. His late boss had bought the fancy-looking sign, which was hidden from sight among numerous miscellaneous items on the shelf. Not once had it ever been hung out, as far as Sentaro could remember.

Wondering if perhaps they had not prepared enough bean paste, he went over the cooking notes with their detailed amounts. But it was the same as always, plus the rubbish bin next to the grill was almost full to overflowing with broken eggshells as further testament. He hurriedly checked the takings. That day he had sold roughly three hundred dorayaki: a record for him.

There was nothing for it but to close for the day. Sentaro pulled down the shutters and set off along the street now bathed in the rays of the setting sun. He headed straight for the soba-noodle shop and a drink. Though tired, he felt a glow of satisfaction. He had not chosen to do this work because he wanted to; he wanted to be free of it as soon as possible. That's all he was aiming for. And yet, he felt a sense of achievement from today, as if he'd turned a corner. That's what puzzled him; this feeling he had of wanting to cheer, along with a sense that things had become somehow complicated. He didn't know where he stood any more.

What was he going to do from now on? This was a question that required urgent consideration. Sentaro pondered as he poured himself a drink.

Should he be resigned to keep hanging up the 'Sold Out' sign, or should he see this as an opportunity and extend business hours into the evening? Whichever course he decided on, Sentaro felt there was something to be said for either option.

If sales kept improving he could make more money, and that would mean he could increase his debt repayments to the owner. Yet a part of him was still prepared to give it up. It was hard to imagine pushing himself any harder than he was already. He did nothing else all day except make dorayaki. Time would pass doing exactly the same thing over and over.

And yet – Sentaro considered the other option – working morning to night was bound to speed up his release from being chained to the grill. In which case, shouldn't he do his utmost to work and save money? Isn't that why the gods had sent him the old lady? He was getting top-class bean paste for rubbish pay – if that wasn't an opportunity, what was?

'Is it time?' he murmured.

His mind spinning drunkenly, Sentaro proceeded to map out a detailed plan. As shopping streets went, Cherry Blossom Street might be down on its heels, but it did get a good flow of human traffic. Peak time was in the evenings, when commuters returning home swelled the ranks of evening shoppers. There were baked-confectionery shops in the city centre that did all their preparation in the daytime and opened from evening until late at night. Why shouldn't he do the same? A surprising number of office workers and business men and women craved something sweet after an evening out drinking with their colleagues. Clearly it was not smart to shut up shop while it was still light, but if he was going to get new customers then he had to stay open until the evening rush was over, which meant keeping the shop open until at least eight or nine at night...Who would make all the extra bean paste that would require?

This was the wall Sentaro ran up against. He didn't think it was possible for a 76-year old woman who sat down at the drop of a hat to work any harder than she already was.

9

Could they increase their sweet bean paste production?

A few days later Sentaro sounded out Tokue. She gave no sign of surprise. Her response was to simply stare at him in silence for a while, and say, 'Good for you.' Her eyes creased in a smile.

'I've got more customers than ever, thanks to you.'

'Are you going to make more bean paste?'

'Yes, soon.'

'In that case I'd better help you.'

Tokue gave no sign of displeasure about an increased workload. After discussing it they decided to increase production to ten-kilogram batches each time.

'We'll be even busier,' Sentaro warned.

'What of it, it's a good thing.'

'How's your health? Will you be able to cope?'

'You'll do all the heavy work, won't you, boss?'

'Yeah, sure.'

'In that case, why don't we start today?' Tokue rocked on her heels, like a young mother holding a baby on her hip.

For the first time ever, Sentaro understood what it was to be truly under pressure at work. On busy days there was no time to even stretch as he stood in front of the griddle all day long, pouring batter onto the grill to cook the pancakes. In between he would see to customers, work the till, and fill the pancakes with sweet bean paste.

As always, he did not take any regular day off, nor did he increase the days Tokue worked. Sentaro kept working, glued to the grill from early morning until night. And so the days went by. Daily takings were consistently good, even with the usual ups and downs.

Before long the misty, drizzly days of the early summer rainy season arrived. Tiny droplets of moisture gathered on the gleaming, deep-green leaves of the cherry trees.

While this may have been good news for the trees, it was not welcome to a confectioner. For Sentaro, who made fresh dorayaki without using preservatives, it signalled the arrival of a trying period. The coarse sweet bean paste used for dorayaki was susceptible to heat and humidity, and could spoil in as little as half a day in the worst conditions. Other types with a higher sugar concentration, such as that used in *monaka*, would keep better.

Sentaro had to be extra careful with the pancakes as well. If he made too many at once and too much time went by before they were consumed, they became sticky and unusable. The only way to avoid this was to

45

try and anticipate the number of customers and cook up small batches at a time. Everything was much more effort during the rainy season.

Nevertheless, Doraharu was still on a roll, thanks to Tokue's bean paste. Customers continued to queue outside the window even while holding an umbrella with one hand. During the same period in previous years there were so few customers the shop might as well have been closed. This year, however, the days went by in a busy blur for Sentaro.

It was around this time that Sentaro began to get dizzy spells as he stood in front of the griddle. In addition to being rushed off his feet all the time, the oppressive summer heat was beginning to take its toll.

The heavy, humid air peculiar to this time of year wormed its way into the shop through the window that was always open for customers. The air conditioner was running constantly, but since Sentaro was always standing next to the heat of the gas-lit griddle, dark patches of sweat stained his apron and clothes. He began to drink large volumes of water while cooking. His appetite naturally decreased and he stopped eating even so much as a sandwich from the convenience store. Still he continued to work without rest, as if possessed.

Nor did the uncomfortable rainy season deter the customers. Finally there came a day when even the increased production was insufficient and Sentaro had to hang out the 'Sold Out' sign once more. He had never felt more tired and worn out in his life. Once back in his flat he collapsed on the kitchen floor and remained prone without moving for a long while. Only after downing copious amounts of whisky did he stretch out on his futon to sleep.

The next morning saw him sitting slumped on a chair in the kitchen of Doraharu. A batch of bean paste that he had made himself was in the copper pot, steeping in syrup, and nearly ready. All he had to do was divide it up and mix a portion in with Tokue's bean paste to make it go further. But Sentaro couldn't move. Though he knew what he had to do next, his body would not respond. He sat there, frozen in the cool blast of air streaming from the air conditioner. It was too much effort even to move his fingers.

That day, Sentaro did not open for business.

At some point he fell asleep sitting up, and when he opened his eyes again the hands of the clock showed it was close to midday. He managed to lift himself from his seat finally but no matter how he tried, could not bring himself to open the shutters. His breathing came in shallow gasps as he wrapped up the bean paste. Before he could put it in the refrigerator he slumped into the chair once again.

Finally gathering up the energy to move, Sentaro changed out of his work clothes and left the shop. Though it had been overcast in the morning when he arrived, a strong glare now reflected off the road surface. Flinching from the strong sunshine, Sentaro sought the shade of a cherry tree.

A cicada chirruped and flew off.

As he stood with both hands pressed against the rough bark of the tree, it was all he could do to remain upright. An uncomfortable sweat streamed from every pore in his body. Surrendering his weight against the trunk, he gazed up at the deep-green treetop and focused on keeping his eyes fixed on the leaves swaying in the wind.

A flickering image of his mother's face floated out from the shadow of the leaves. She had visited him when he was in prison, but had always remained silent, her face through the clear acrylic barrier looking more aged with each visit.

All of a sudden Sentaro felt like weeping. With tears threatening to spill over, he headed for the road along the train line to avoid the shopping street where people might see him. Upon reaching the road he stopped and watched several trains go by. There seemed no way forward, or back. After a while he became scared of his thoughts in that place and set off walking toward a residential area.

Bright sunshine poured down from a clear sky. In Sentaro's mind the clarity of the day only highlighted his state of wretchedness. All the time he had ever squandered in his life seemed to be clinging to his footsteps, dragging him down. He felt as if he were a scrap of rubbish, drifting through one backstreet alley after another.

Die, he thought he heard a voice whisper.

By the time he returned to his flat he had wandered so long and so far he had no memory of where exactly he had been.

He flopped down on the futon still laid out on the floor. His chest gave off a dull heat, as if the blood was pooling there.

Die. Wouldn't it be better to die?

Sentaro felt himself sink and be drawn in by that voice. He was drowning, and his breath was shallow. He fell into a feverish dream. Gasping and drenched in sweat, he struggled in an unfamiliar place.

IO

The phone was ringing.

Sentaro lifted his head and saw light behind the curtains. The clock showed that it was eight in the morning. Sentaro couldn't work out why the telephone was hounding him, and why the room was bright to begin with. The ringing persisted. He crawled over to the kitchen to pick up the receiver.

'Boss, what's wrong?' Tokue was on the other end.

Sentaro mumbled something vaguely and she asked again, 'What's wrong?'

'Well...'

'Are you all right?'

He saw a flashback of railway tracks and felt cherry-tree bark under his palms.

'Well, I...'

His hazy mind started to turn. He had given Tokue a copy of the shop key in case of emergency. She must have opened up by herself and started work.

'Did you oversleep? Or don't you feel well?'

'Sorry.' He meant to say he would be there soon, but the words stuck in his throat. 'I'm a bit under the weather,' he came out with.

'What's wrong?'

'I think— I'm probably tired.'

'Will you be all right?'

'I might have a rest today.'

Tokue paused. 'Well it's no wonder, you've been working nonstop,' she said. 'That's a good idea.'

'I'm sorry.'

'I already started cooking the bean paste, so I'll leave when it's done.'

'Sorry. Will you be okay on your own?'

'I'll be fine. You worry about yourself. Why don't you take two or three days—?'

'I'll be in tomorrow,' he cut Tokue short. If he stayed away that long Sentaro felt he was likely to never go back. 'When you've finished today's batch, please go home.'

'Yes, all right. I'll do that, but...' Tokue hesitated.

'I'm sorry, just do as I ask please,' Sentaro ordered and hung up before she could reply.

The next morning Sentaro set out for Doraharu earlier than usual. When he arrived, however, he found the shutters already half-open and a sweet aroma in the air.

'Tokue?'

'Oh, boss.'

'Tokue, what are you doing here so early?'

'I thought I'd make the bean paste instead of you.'

'You...*what*?'

Sentaro could not absorb this: Tokue was here,

starting work by herself, on a day when she was not scheduled to come in.

'Thank you,' he said with a nod.

'How are you today?'

Tokue looked up from the beans she was watching over as they boiled away in the pot, and flashed a smile at Sentaro.

'I think I'm okay now.'

'It's not right you don't take any time off,' she said.

'Yes, well, I'll think about it.'

Sentaro threaded his arms through the sleeves of his chef's coat as he spoke, but when it came to doing up the buttons his fingers suddenly stopped. Yesterday on the phone Tokue had said that she was starting to make bean paste, which meant that there should be enough for today. So why was she here again this morning making more?

'Tokue, didn't you make bean paste yesterday? Where is it?'

'Ah yes, yesterday, err...'

She lifted her eyes from the pot but did not immediately look at Sentaro directly. Then she shrugged and turned to face him.

'Well now, you see, I didn't know what to do. I made the bean paste and was just sitting down for a little rest, when a customer arrived.'

'Huh?'

'Yes, a customer came and, so...I had to open the shop.'

'Huh? What?' Sentaro's head jerked forward in shock.

'You opened the shop? But...how did you open the shutters?'

'You know I never liked the shutters all closed up, so I just opened the bottom part, like you see now, and that's when a customer called out to me.'

'But you promised. You said you'd go home after finishing the bean paste.' Sentaro felt the sweat forming in his armpits. 'What about the pancakes?'

'Oh, I cooked those too.'

'You did what? You were able to cook them?'

'Oh, I managed somehow. I'm sorry, boss.'

'It's a bit late for sorry.'

Tokue put the wooden spatula down and pointed at the countertop.

'I didn't know how you do your books, so I just wrote how much I sold in there.'

'Who asked you to—?'

It was a simple table. Figures for the day's takings and profit were recorded in the distinctive curling handwriting Sentaro knew. The numbers were impressive.

'Did you do this all by yourself?'

'It was very busy. Customers didn't stop coming.'

'And you really did this all alone?'

'Yes, by myself. Oh, but the first customer helped with the shutters. And I asked the last customer to help me close them.'

Sentaro felt like sitting down in shock. How had she managed it? What was her pancake batter like? She had handled all the money with those gnarled fingers...? What had the customers thought of that?!

'I'm sorry,' Tokue repeated.

'Ah...I'm just surprised, that's all. You could've said something.'

'But you would've said no, wouldn't you?'

Clearly she'd broken the rules, but Sentaro recognized he was in no position to reprimand her for it. Tokue shifted her grip on the wooden spatula and stood there stiffly, like a child who's been scolded.

'But, I can't imagine...You must've been exhausted after selling all that.'

'Yes. I was very tired.'

'And then you came in early today.'

'Yes. I was here early.'

Unsure of what attitude he should adopt, Sentaro instead slapped his own cheek. Tokue flinched but Sentaro paid no heed and picked up the measuring cup.

'Boss...'

'That's enough. How many kilograms of adzuki are we cooking today?'

'Let me see...two kilograms of dried beans.'

Sentaro did the sums in his head and poured the sugar for the syrup onto the scales.

'Boss?'

'Yeah.'

'Why'd you do that? Were you trying to get your-self moving?

'No, that's not it.' Sentaro didn't understand him-self why he'd slapped his own cheek.

Tokue was in high spirits all that day. She chattered away while stirring the beans with the wooden spatula.

'Boss, where are you from?'

'Takasaki.'

'Have you been in Tokyo ever since you left?'

'Well, I've moved around a bit.'

'Really? Lucky you,' Tokue sighed in envy.

'It's not that great. I just sort of...bounced around.'

'Is that so? Whereabouts?'

'Oh, just the Kanto region.'

'Well that's not so bad, is it? I err...I lived in Aichi Prefecture when I was a child.'

'Aichi?'

'Yes. In real countryside. On the Iida Line out from Toyohashi.'

Tokue lifted her eyes away from the beans – some-thing she would ordinarily never do – and looked at Sentaro.

'The cherry blossoms there were *so* beautiful.'

'Oh, where did you say it was again?'

'Ah, um...' She hesitated. 'There was a cliff, with a river at the bottom. And the slope from the cliff to the river was covered with cherry trees. I've never seen any as beautiful as those.'

For some reason Tokue did not name the place.

'Do you go back there sometimes?'

Tokue shook her head. 'No, I haven't been back for decades.' She turned her eyes back to the beans in the pot.

'What kind of food do you like, boss? What's the local specialty in Takasaki?'

'Let me see...Daruma *bento* is about all I can think of. You know, the boxed lunches you can buy at the train station.'

Sentaro smiled as he filled the stockpot with water for the syrup. Tokue sounded like a child. He was grateful just to pass the time answering her undemanding questions.

'Daruma lunchboxes come in white or red,' he said. 'I wonder if it's because there's something different inside.'

'I like the sound of station lunchboxes, and eating while you travel.'

'What do you like to eat, Tokue? Food simmered in miso's a specialty in Aichi, isn't it? Or those flat *kishimen* noodles.'

'We didn't have anything so nice when I was growing up,' she said, flapping her hands as if to wave away the very idea. 'When I say countryside, I mean real country. We used to pickle cherry-blossom petals and put them in hot water to drink.'

'Wow, sounds like a foreign country.'

'Japan then and now are different countries.'

Sentaro nodded and put the stockpot on the gas. 'Anything and everything changes, doesn't it?'

'Like what?' Tokue looked Sentaro up and down.

'Like...me.'

'What?'

'Well...I'm in debt. To the owner of this shop. The wife of my late boss.'

'Oh, my.'

'I don't know what to say. There was a time when I went off the rails a bit.'

'You owe money? Are you sure you're not being cheated?'

'It's okay. The boss took care of my debts. That's why I'm here. I'm still repaying the money to his wife.' Sentaro glanced at Tokue. 'Keep your eye on the pot.'

She hastily turned back to stare into the copper bean pot again. 'But how did you get into debt?'

Sentaro looked into the stockpot and saw tiny bubbles dancing on the bottom.

'I'm embarrassed to say, but I didn't always keep to the straight and narrow. I just bumbled along, not knowing what to do with my life, really. Whatever I did never worked out. At one time I wanted to be a writer. But I never write a word these days. I never became expert in dorayaki either. I'm just a waster.'

'But you work hard now. You never take time off.'

'Hah.'

Tokue turned off the flame under the pot of beans but made no move to start rinsing. She stared at the boiled beans.

'Let's make a go of it together, you and me,' she said, turning to look Sentaro in the eye. 'I'll help you.'

The stockpot in front of Sentaro started to boil.

'It's okay. You do enough already. With you around I feel like I have an ally. Fate can be a tough deal.' Sentaro went to pick up the cup of sugar.

'Fate?' Tokue's voice was charged. 'What do you mean? Don't throw around words like fate, Sentaro.'

'Huh?'

'Young people shouldn't talk about fate.'

Chastised, Sentaro looked at the floor.

'I...there was a period when I couldn't leave the same place for a long time,' Tokue said, and quickly shook her head, as if the words that had slipped out were somehow distasteful. She began to fill the copper bean pot with water.

'I'm sorry. I appreciate your concern.'

'I'm sorry, too,' she said, not meeting Sentaro's eye. 'Please forget about it.'

II

Summer arrived in full force. Cicadas cried from the cherry trees and in the evenings a pleasant breeze blew briefly as dusk began to arrive earlier each day.

At Doraharu, Sentaro was set to get through the summer period without any seasonal slump in business. Custom from school kids usually dropped off during the summer holidays, but that wasn't happening this year. Quite the opposite, in fact, for the young girls continued to gather there every day at the counter seats. They came for dorayaki and cold drinks, and, to Sentaro's surprise, Tokue's presence also seemed to be a draw.

The group of girls who stopped by on their way home from cram school were in that category. They'd sit at the counter with their heads propped on their hands, and complain in voices loud enough for Tokue to hear from where she was sitting on her chair in the back.

'Study is a pain in the neck,' one might say.

And with a smile Tokue would reply from her seat, 'Well then, why don't you take a day off and have some fun?'

The girls wrinkled up their noses at that. 'My parents would throw me out.'

'Leave then. If you want to have fun.'

'Seriously?'

'I'm serious.'

'Ooooh, are you telling us to be delinquents?'

Sentaro could see that while keeping her distance, Tokue appeared to wait for the right timing to deliver her comments. Whenever she heard their loud voices coming up the street, she would retreat dolefully to the seat in the back, but there would already be a vague smile on her face.

'Home is *sooo* boring. I don't wanna go back!' wailed one girl.

'Why don't you find something to do with yourself?' Tokue instantly responded.

'Like what?' the girl asked.

'What about working here part-time?' Tokue proposed.

'Stop that now,' Sentaro shot back from in front of the griddle. He was afraid she was only half-joking.

Granted these were school kids, but it was a problem for him that they stuck around two hours or so only for the price of one dorayaki. It was on the tip of his tongue to suggest they must be tired of chattering and how about getting a move on. He didn't appreciate Tokue butting in and keeping their conversation going.

But ever since the day she had run the shop by herself, Sentaro had changed his tune. He let her do as she pleased. She was there on a pitifully low wage, and her presence in the shop was part of the reckoning. Which was not to say, however, that he thought it acceptable to lower all barriers between them and the customers.

There was something else that bothered Sentaro: the expressions on customers' faces when they caught sight of Tokue sitting in the back. These included the school girls. He had not missed the way some of them looked at her and suddenly lapsed into silence, or the momentary flash in their eyes.

There was one school girl who mostly came alone. Her name was Wakana, which was a nickname, and she never said how it originated. According to the other girls, there was a time when Wakana wore her hair short in a cute bob, just like the well-known cartoon character Wakame-chan, so maybe that explained it. But after court proceedings and her parents' divorce, neither Wakana's personality nor her hairstyle had ever been the same, apparently.

Wakana was not a talkative girl. She would sit and eat dorayaki while staring into the kitchen with dewy eyes. That gaze bothered Sentaro, who sometimes asked – unusually for him – if she was all right.

But Wakana always kept quiet, even when Sentaro spoke to her. It was only after Tokue began giving her the misshapen reject dorayaki that she started to speak of her own accord. She mentioned that she lived with just her mother, who worked at night, that money was tight, and that she would come home after school to find her mother's boyfriend's underwear lying about the house.

Tokue sometimes gave reject dorayaki to the other girls too when they chatted with her. She would take the pancakes that Sentaro had spoiled during cooking, put sweet bean paste or cream in them, and give them to the girls, saying, 'This is on the house.'

Sentaro did not like her doing this. He tried to tell her so indirectly but she dismissed him. 'What's wrong with it?' she said. 'Better than throwing them away.'

Wakana said the rejects tasted better than the standard dorayaki. This spurred Tokue on to try honey and other fillings. It was after polishing off one of these experiments one day that Wakana finally brought up the so-far-unmentioned.

'Tokue, what happened to your fingers?'

Sentaro turned around to see Tokue, who was seated, fold her hands in an attempt to hide her fingers.

'Oh, this. When I was a girl I got sick and my fingers stayed crooked.'

'What kind of sickness?'

He saw her expression harden.

'An awful sickness,' was all she said.

Wakana nodded and said nothing more. She bit into her remaining dorayaki and chewed without comment, as if to cover the awkwardness of the moment. To Sentaro her chewing sounded like a wordless conversation between Tokue and Wakana.

From that day on Wakana did not come to Doraharu any more.

Tokue often chatted about the students while she did the washing-up. She noted how so-and-so had recently started to smile, so things must be better at home. Or how she thought somebody else probably had a broken heart because she'd seen the girl's friends consoling her. The things people said in that situation never changed with the times, she observed. Another girl had shown Tokue her new mobile phone, which was apparently the very latest, so Sentaro probably hadn't seen one yet either, she said. What kind of world will it be in the future now that those things are an inseparable part of children's lives, she wondered.

Tokue also mentioned Wakana. 'She hasn't been by recently,' she said one day.

Sentaro was scraping the burnt crumbs off the griddle. 'You mean that rude girl?'

'Why do you say that?'

'She sprung that question about your fingers on you, didn't she?'

'You were the same,' Tokue stated.

'It was my job to say that. I had to ask at least once.'

'But...that's how it is.'

'Huh?' Sentaro looked confused.

'I sometimes think...well, what of it?'

Sentaro raised his eyes from the griddle to look at

Tokue, still not understanding.

'Only adults look while pretending not to. Is that better? Or is it better to ask straight out?'

'Ah, difficult question.'

'I could tell Wakana had been wondering about my fingers for a while. She only asked because she wanted to know me better.'

'You think so?'

'Yes, so don't pick on that girl or talk about her like that.'

'What's this? Now you're angry at me?'

Tokue smiled and Sentaro relaxed slightly. 'You like children, don't you?' he said. 'Me, I get uptight when they come here in groups.'

'I wanted to be a teacher, you know.'

'Primary school?'

'That would've been all right, but mostly I wanted to teach Japanese at middle school. I wanted to study, you know.'

'I guess things were hard after the war, the country was poor.' Instinctively Sentaro tried to anticipate Tokue, and create a space for her words.

'Everybody was poor, not just my family.'

'Why a Japanese teacher?' Sentaro kept the questions coming, trying to mend things.

'I liked poetry. I used to read poetry when I was young. Like Heine and Hakushu Kitahara and other poets, in books I found in my older brother's room.'

'Goodness, Tokue. You're full of surprises.'

'Reading and imagining things was about the only pleasure we had in those days. I loved using my imagination. That's why I thought it interesting you wanted to be a writer.'

'That was a long time ago.'

'But don't you still have dreams from the past? I never thought I'd get the chance in this life to talk with sweet young girls like that. That's why I'm so happy.'

'By sweet, you mean those girls that come here?'

'Yes, I do. I never got to be a teacher, but now I can enjoy a fraction of what it might've been like. Thank you, for giving me the chance to meet those girls.'

'Get on with you. I'm the one who's being helped.'

As he scrubbed the griddle with a scouring brush, Sentaro silently prayed for Wakana to show her face again soon.

12

Summer holidays came to an end and the girls who gathered at Doraharu began appearing in their school uniforms again. The days were still hot and humid, but as evening drew near, the air cooled considerably. Faded leaves rustled in the wind and fell one by one to the footpath outside the shop.

Sentaro had finished cleaning inside and was removing dead leaves from the shutter grooves when he heard a voice behind him. 'Sorry to come at this late hour.' It was his boss, the owner.

'Oh,' he uttered in surprise, 'Madam.'

He ushered her inside to a counter seat. Sentaro was rattled by this unscheduled visit, and searched his mind, trying to think why she might be here. They met every week for her to check the books and bank transfers – sometimes at the shop and sometimes at her home – but it was always prearranged. She was surprisingly busy with all her medical appointments. Sentaro, too, was always working, so it wasn't as if he had a lot of time either. Any business matters were therefore usually discussed out of shop hours when there were no customers, and she always telephoned the day before.

It suited Sentaro to have this tacit understanding as it gave him time to get the books in order and clean before she came. Most importantly, however, he could make sure that Tokue was not around.

So why, now, all of a sudden...? Sentaro had a bad feeling. Tokue had been in the shop just a short while before, doing the washing-up. Had the owner arrived an hour earlier they would have run into each other.

She put her stick on the counter. 'Tea please, Sentaro,' she said, pointing to the cups. He put the kettle on the stove.

'Sorry to come when you're busy.'

'Not at all. What's up?'

Her eyes darted about the interior then abruptly she pursed her lips and looked Sentaro in the eye.

'There are rumours,' she began, 'about someone who works here.'

'Oh, that would be Tokue.'

'Tokue – is that her name?'

The moment Sentaro had feared was finally here. He looked away and put his fingers on the kettle handle.

'I heard about it from somebody. Is it true her hands are crippled?'

Sentaro closed his eyes once before speaking. 'Err, a little bit...Is that a problem?'

'And is her face paralysed as well?'

Sentaro gave her a puzzled look.

'My friend says – I'm sorry, but this is not good – my friend says it looks like leprosy.'

'Leprosy?'

'Nowadays they call it Hansen's disease.'

'Hansen's disease...' Sentaro felt the blood drain from his face.

'Yes, and that got me worried. Actually, I came by here an hour ago and watched from the road.'

'Why'd you do that? You could've come inside and met Tokue directly.'

She nodded and gave Sentaro a steely look. 'That wouldn't be very good for you, would it, Sentaro? Haven't you been sneaking about up to now, making sure I didn't meet her?'

'Huh? No...what do you mean?'

The kettle vibrated under his hand as the water approached the boil. Inside he felt even more turbulent.

'I couldn't see very well, but there was definitely something wrong with that woman's hands.'

'Not so much that you notice it.'

'The customers notice. It's not good for the shop.'

'Hah...'

'If there's something you're not telling me, spit it out.'

'That's not...I just want to say this shop has been turned around because of Tokue's bean paste. She has fifty years' experience of making it.'

Sentaro didn't wait for the kettle to come to the boil. He poured water into the teapot.

'She's popular with the young people too.'

'Oh really. She obviously works hard.'

'Yes. She does a good job.'

'How old is this person?'

'In her seventies,' Sentaro answered, pouring tea into a cup, 'but she's very good for her age.' He smiled at the owner.

'About the same age as me,' she said, taking the cup. 'Ugh!' she drew a sharp breath.

'What is it?'

'Did she use this cup too?'

He nodded.

'They say it's rarely catching...Sentaro, this is serious. What if it gets out that an eating establishment is employing a leprosy patient?'

'But...Tokue got sick when she was a girl, and her fingers went like that as a side effect. She's been cured for a long time now.'

'She would say that, wouldn't she? Did you know, Sentaro, that in severe cases of leprosy the fingers drop off?'

'Tokue has all her fingers.'

'Where does she live? That woman.'

Sentaro turned away and put a hand against his chest, as if to still the turmoil. The notebook in which Tokue had written her address was on a shelf in the kitchen. He found it and opened it up for the owner to see. She looked at the writing, went still and closed her eyes.

'What is it?'

'This is where they keep the lepers.' Her voice was

a whisper though no one else was present. 'There's a sanatorium.'

Sentaro put both hands on the countertop. In silence, he looked at the address Tokue had written. So that was it. That's why it had triggered something the first time he saw it. At the time he couldn't figure out why, but now it was mentioned he remembered that he'd heard rumours about this district before, because of the sanatorium.

'This writing is all crooked.'

'But— She says she's cured.'

'I don't know about now, Sentaro, but people used to get put in isolation for life when they got that disease. I saw them when I was a girl, hanging around the temple. Their faces looked dreadful – like monsters. The public-health authorities used to disinfect any place they'd been.'

'But madam...' Sentaro picked up the cup that she had pushed back towards him and took it over to the sink. 'I know I've said it already, but it's because of Tokue this place is making a profit at last. She comes here early and makes bean paste for me.'

The owner looked shrewdly at the copper bean pot sitting on the gas cooker and the bowl with adzuki beans soaking in it.

'I can see that. But if the person who informed me starts talking to others, we're done for. What if somebody around here got leprosy and this shop was the source of infection?'

'Who told you *what*, exactly?'

'I can't tell you that.' She clamped her lips and stared at Sentaro.

'Think what will happen if she stays here. What if you catch it too?'

Sentaro could only blink in reply. He turned to look at the soaking beans.

'In any case... Tokue, is it? You have to—' She broke off, then continued to wind up her case. 'You can pay her off – give her a good sum – but you have to let her go. If she doesn't, this place will fold.'

'But what will I do for bean paste?'

'You can make it, can't you? You must've learned by now if you've been making it with her.'

Had he? Sentaro was not confident. He was still continually amazed by Tokue's attitude towards the beans. At a deep level, she was doing something very different to him.

'Well, Sentaro? Can't you make the bean paste yourself?'

'That's not the problem.'

'What, then?'

'The thing is, Tokue and I have made this shop profitable together. We even get queues sometimes. There're kids who depend on her, too. Is that the kind of person you want me to fire?'

'I don't like having to say this either, you know. But it can't be helped. This is a disease we're talking about. A very serious one. And at least one person has already noticed.'

71

Sentaro could see she was not going to budge. Though he did not refuse to obey her outright, he was careful to say, 'Please give me some time.'

The owner looked annoyed. 'You promised to let me be there when you interviewed casual workers,' she said insistently, and pointed to a corner of the kitchen. 'Give me that,' she said, thrusting her chin in the direction of the alcohol sterilizing spray for kitchen use.

Sentaro passed it over and she sprayed it on her hands. Fine beads of alcohol solution hung in the air, and floated over to the beans Tokue had left soaking.

'I understand how you might feel. I don't enjoy saying this. But sacrifices are sometimes necessary. My husband entrusted this shop to you. You're in charge of it so I want you to do the job properly and not let your emotions carry you away. And besides...' she paused, 'don't you still owe us money?'

Sentaro lowered his eyes and said nothing. He didn't lift his face again until she had gone.

That night Sentaro could not sleep.

Unusually for him, he went to bed without a drink, and stared up at the dark ceiling, his mind in a whirl. After a while he reached the conclusion that he knew nothing about Hansen's disease and pushed back the covers, since he couldn't sleep. Switching on the light at the desk, he started up an ancient, dust-covered computer for the first time in a while and connected it to the internet with an analogue cable that had also been lying around disused. Once it was set up he typed 'hansens disease' into a search engine.

A list of article titles appeared on the screen. Sentaro stared at the monitor, not knowing where to start. All he knew was that he did not want to look at shocking photographs of patients. Girding himself to get on with it, he started off by reading through all the titles in order. The content seemed widely varied: historical accounts of the illness, medical explanations, the bittersweet victories and struggles of former patients who had fought for the repeal of the Leprosy Prevention Act, digests from major newspapers, and relevant pages on the Ministry of Health website.

He chose a selection and looked through them methodically. Every article contained medical terms that made the topic seem difficult, but he was able to glean enough by reading the more accessible parts and piecing all the information together.

To begin with, he discovered that everybody currently living in sanatoriums around Japan was cured of the disease. There were no current patients. And in the unlikely case that there was an outbreak of Hansen's, modern methods of treatment were capable of quickly achieving a complete cure with no further possibility of the patient being contagious to others. Moreover, the disease had an extremely low degree of infectivity, and apparently no Japanese medical staff had ever contracted it in the course of administering treatment.

In the days of less advanced hygiene, however, when treatment methods were yet to be established, it was regarded as an incurable disease, and patients were therefore quarantined by law. They also suffered from discrimination because of side effects that caused parts of the body to drop off. But such symptoms were only evident in patients who had not received treatment until the disease was far advanced. With early and appropriate treatment, there were no permanent side effects.

After skimming through once more, Sentaro shut down the computer. He had seen photographs that made him want to turn his eyes away, but the problem of Tokue weighed less heavily on him now. There were still sanatoriums, it was true, but no more patients, and most importantly, there were no carriers any more.

Even if Tokue had suffered from this disease in the past, as the owner suspected, there should be no issue about it now. To say nothing of the fact that Tokue had said she got it when she was young. A long time would have passed since she was completely cured.

He didn't need to make Tokue leave. Although Sentaro was convinced of this now, he was still not sure how to handle the situation.

Sentaro contemplated printing out some of the articles he'd read on the internet and showing them to the owner. The disease had been all but eradicated in Japan so it was simply not possible that Tokue could be a source of contagion decades after being cured.

Should he point that out to her? He was not confident, however, that such a direct approach would cut any ice with her. Simply saying that, medically speaking, there was nothing to worry about, would not undo the damage done to Tokue's fingers by the disease. And her fingers were what people saw. Sentaro had a feeling the owner would not change her mind about wanting Tokue gone.

In which case, what should he do?

It dawned on him that one way out might be to get Tokue to leave temporarily. It would be a stretch, to be sure, but he could tell her this had been a temporary position and ask her to leave, then ask her back when the timing was good, to continue teaching him how to make bean paste. Sentaro thought it through. He could smooth things over with the owner and do his best in the meantime to hone his own sweet bean paste making skills.

But the more he thought about it, the less enthusiasm Sentaro had for the idea. He would just be going through the motions and could not think of any reason he could give Tokue as to why she must quit. Besides, he was the one who wanted to get away from the shop. Was it even necessary for him to stick around to deal with this problem?

Sentaro continued staring at the dark ceiling, unable to reach a conclusion.

13

In the end Sentaro could not come to any decision.

Unable to decide on any course of action regarding Tokue, or the future of the shop, he simply continued to work as usual. He said nothing to Tokue of the owner's visit, or what he had read on the internet about Hansen's disease. Nor did he change his attitude toward her in any way. Sentaro just went on as usual. However, anxiety lay heavy in the pit of his stomach. It was only a matter of time before the owner would demand an explanation, and he had to work out how he was going to placate her when the time came.

It was all getting too much. Sentaro asked himself if he should quit too. He thought about abandoning everything, but then recalled his late boss's square face. 'I'll take care of your money problems, come and help me out.'

Sentaro had been working part-time in a pub after his release from prison when the big man had approached him with this offer.

He had been imprisoned for a direct violation of the Cannabis Control Act. It was his first offence, but he had also been involved in trafficking. Although he wasn't the prime culprit, he had ties with the fringes of an organized-crime group, from which he received certain financial benefits. His sentence reflected this, with no suspension, and he ended up staring at the walls for two years. During the course of a tough interrogation leading up to this, he never divulged the names of certain people. His former boss was one of them; a small-time, shady character who traded on his links with criminal gangs. But to Sentaro there was still human warmth in the man.

'You did good, protecting me,' he'd said the night Sentaro told him he would work at Doraharu. The two had been standing on the roadside, the big man weeping silently. Then they went drinking until morning.

The boss suffered from cirrhosis due to long years of heavy drinking. His face was the same bronze colour as the dorayaki he cooked. In the end he vomited up blood while in the middle of pulling on his shoes to go to the hospital, and passed away on the spot from a burst vein. That was when Sentaro was in his third year of helping out at Doraharu.

After the funeral, his wife pleaded with Sentaro to stay on at the shop. Her husband had told her to leave things to him if something happened, she said, clasping both his hands in hers and with tears in her eyes.

It was true this couple had helped him during an unsettled period in his life after his release from prison. When Sentaro thought about it like that, leaving the shop before he'd finished paying back his debts was inconceivable. He understood that very well.

He sighed as he stood at the griddle thinking it over. What a dilemma. It wasn't as if he was a regular hard-working guy to begin with. What the hell should he do?

Unable to find any answer, Sentaro simply kept on doing what he did every day: cooking pancakes for dorayaki, filling them with bean paste and smiling for the customers. And like his late boss, he drank, night after night.

Time went by and the autumnal rain front arrived, bringing day after day of unending drizzle. Passers-by were now wearing warm cardigans and jackets, and carried umbrellas in one hand. The faded leaves on the tree outside the shop began dropping constantly.

The change came suddenly. By the time Sentaro noticed, it was already significant.

'Is it the rain, I wonder,' he muttered with a concerned expression, as he and Tokue looked over the books together.

They had to adjust the volume of beans they cooked. In fact, there was already a plentiful supply of bean paste in the refrigerator, and no need to cook any more. For some reason, sales had fallen over the last week, and the last three days in particular had been terrible.

Tokue looked through the window up at the leaden sky and then at the road. 'If only the weather'd clear up a bit.'

'This weather is enough to get anyone down,' Sentaro said, trying to dispel a niggling, unvoiced anxiety.

The drop in takings was unmistakable. Slowly but surely sales had fallen, as if in tandem with the ever-shortening days.

'Things will pick up when the rain stops,' he said, as if reassuring himself.

'Yes, all we need is a bit of blue sky.'

In his heart Sentaro suspected there might be another reason. Given the busy period during the rainy season back in June, this explanation didn't make sense. Customers had lined up in the rain, holding umbrellas, in spite of the heat and humidity, and sales had grown. So what was going on now? Ordinarily, this should be the start of the season for dorayaki, when the air began to feel cool on the skin.

He also considered that perhaps the sluggish economy had something to do with it. There were permanently shuttered shops all around them on this street. Just last week a fishmonger had closed up, a business that had managed to struggle along for many years. It was getting more and more deserted around here. Weather like this, when the rain set in and the sky was overcast day after day, was enough to make anyone depressed. Nobody would feel like buying anything, would they?

'Come to think of it, I haven't bought anything recently either.' Tokue, who had been staring vaguely out the window, turned and looked at him as if to say, what are you talking about?

'How about you, Tokue? Have you bought anything recently?'

She still didn't appear to grasp his train of thought and the significance of what she was being asked. 'You mean go shopping?' she answered.

'Yeah. We aren't selling much, but then I was thinking, well, we're not buying anything either.'

Tokue nodded, getting his meaning at last. 'I don't really go shopping,' she murmured, and turned her back on Sentaro to retreat into the rear of the shop.

That evening the owner came back, arriving after Tokue had left.

She sat at the counter and looked over the books, saying little, then straightened up with a loud sigh.

'Sentaro.'

Sentaro also straightened up.

'Didn't I ask you to let that woman go as soon as possible?'

Sentaro stood stiff and nodded.

'I've been back several times, keeping my distance even though this is my own shop. You have a reputation to keep up, too, you know. That woman is always here, isn't she? Tokue or whatever her name is. She's still working here.'

'But, in the sense you're talking about...Tokue's all right. Because she's cured.'

'If she's cured why is she still in the sanatorium? Why haven't you done anything about this?'

'I, err...'

'Did you speak to her?'

Sentaro was stuck for words.

'What? Haven't you even asked by now if she's got leprosy?'

'Well...'

'What are you thinking of?!' The owner's voice vibrated shrilly.

'Now, just a moment, madam.'

'And what should I wait for? You've already kept me waiting all this time.'

'Tokue was ill a long time ago, and it might've been Hansen's disease, but she's cured now – she's the same as anyone else.'

'She is not the same! Her fingers are crooked, aren't they?'

'That disease has been as good as eradicated in Japan. There're no patients in the sanatoriums any more.'

'What do you mean? Why should I believe you when you're not a doctor or anything?'

'Are you telling me to fire someone who's not sick, just because she was in the past?'

'This shop serves food and drink! We have an image to protect. Do you think we can have someone here who scares the customers away?'

The owner put her hands to her angry red cheeks, then dropped them to her side.

81

'I didn't want to have to say this, but it's thanks to this shop that you can survive, isn't it? When you had your back to the wall, who was it that took care of things? Surely you don't think Doraharu belongs to you, do you Sentaro? If you don't fire that woman I have no choice but to ask you to leave. Do I make myself clear?'

'But...I, err...'

'My husband started this shop. I am the owner now.'

'Madam.'

'I know. It's not easy for you, either. But look at these figures. How could you do so well and then suddenly this happens? Could it be, by any chance, that rumours have spread about a diseased person working here? If so, this shop is done for.'

'No. If that were the case I would have heard. It's probably this long rainy season. Business is bad everywhere, and it just keeps on raining.'

'Whatever. Just send her packing.' The owner drew in a deep breath and pressed her lips tight. There was a long silence. Apparently, she was waiting for Sentaro to reply, but Sentaro said nothing, and she lost patience. 'That's my last word,' she said, and stormed out of the shop.

14

Crickets chirped beneath the cherry tree. Footsteps clicked distinctly on the road at intervals as people came and went. The stars shone brightly on this quiet autumn night, visible again for the first time in days.

The griddle was already cooling off but Sentaro still had sweat running down his face. 'You won't change your mind?'

Tokue was sitting down. 'No,' she said with a shake of her head. 'I came to this decision by myself. I'm almost at my limit.'

'You could come in just once or twice a month?'

'I don't think...'

'But I still haven't learned everything I need to know about your sweet bean paste.'

Voices filtered through the half-closed shutters. Probably school girls on their way home from after-school activities. A pair of legs in a short skirt appeared below the shutter. 'Looks closed. Aw, that sucks.'

'Sorry. We're finished for today,' Sentaro called out.

He heard a grumble in reply and the sound of retreating footsteps.

'That's the girls who play tennis.' A smile lit Tokue's

eyes for a second then she promptly hung her head again. Her clasped hands rested on the folded apron on her lap.

'Those girls will feel the same as I do. I wish you'd come and visit sometimes,' Sentaro pleaded.

Tokue shook her head.

'Why not, Tokue?'

'I think the reason sales are down recently might be because of my past.'

'Oh, I...I don't think...'

'I'm sure of it.'

'We don't know that.'

'Though I was cured more than forty years ago.'

Then don't quit, Sentaro wanted to say – thought he *should* say, in fact – but he saw the owner's face in his mind and the words died on his lips. He said nothing.

Tokue looked at him with concern. 'Sentaro, it's all right.'

'No, I can't get things right. It's my fault too.'

Tokue picked up the apron from her knees and gripped the hem with her bent fingers. 'Why is it your fault?' she asked.

'Tokue?'

'Yes.'

'I don't think I should have to ask you this, but your sickness...was it Hansen's disease?'

'Yes, it was. I should have told you before.'

'Oh...' Sentaro mumbled vaguely, but could say no more.

'Once you get diagnosed that's the end of your life. That's how it used to be with this sickness.'

Sentaro looked at Tokue's fingers, clutching the hem of her apron.

'Divine punishment, they called it. Some people even said it was punishment for sins in a previous life, you know. If somebody got it, the police and public-health officials were called in, and then there'd be full-on disinfecting. It was awful for families too. They were made to feel terribly ashamed.'

'But you were cured, weren't you?'

Tokue nodded emphatically.

'Yes, we got the medicine from America. But I still got these side effects in my fingers. Other people too.'

'I read a bit about it. Were you really isolated? I mean, like...completely?'

'Yes.' Tokue raised one eyebrow. 'So you did some research?'

'Ah, yes, on the internet.'

'Well, now, complete isolation. It meant we were never allowed outside those gates. It's not so long since that law was abolished, you know.'

'Sorry to harp on about this, but you don't have the disease any more, do you?'

'No. I was diagnosed a non-carrier forty years ago. But I still wasn't allowed to go out into town like this. When I first got sick, I was only...' Tokue's voice trailed off. She pressed her lips together and brought the edge of the apron up to her eyes.

85

'I'm so sorry, Tokue.' Sentaro looked at the floor.

'I was still only about the same age as those young girls that come here.'

At the thought of all she had gone through, Sentaro could not bring himself to look her in the face.

'Tokue...'

'I've been shut up ever since.'

'You've been in a sanatorium all this time?'

'Yes. Tenshoen.'

So that was it. Sentaro realized he had heard the name before. He knew roughly where it was but had never been in the neighbourhood.

'That's quite a way from here, isn't it? How did you get here so early before the buses start running?'

'Oh, that was no problem.'

'Surely not by taxi?'

'I said it's fine.' Tokue smiled wanly.

'You came by taxi...on that pay? I'm sorry.'

'Don't worry. I enjoyed every moment.'

'You don't—'

'No, I mean it. There was a time when I'd given up all hope of ever going outside those gates into the world again. But now look at me. I could come here. I met so many people. All because you gave me a job.'

Sentaro hastily shook his head. 'You're the one who helped me.'

'Oh, get on with you, boss. I'm an old woman. With hands like this. And my face is half-paralyzed too. You took me on in spite of all that. And you let me talk with those sweet girls. I always wanted to do this kind of work, so I'm happy.' Tokue dabbed her eyes with the apron. 'In fact, I've been thinking about quitting. I've been feeling a bit weary recently. It's good timing.' She dipped her white-haired head low in a respectful bow. 'Thank you,' she said.

'No, I'm the one who should thank you. For all you've done for me.'

'Well, I'll be off, then.'

Still seated, Tokue turned to let her gaze travel all around the shop, letting it pause on the plate of reject pancakes. Then she refolded her apron, placed it on the kitchen counter, put her scarf in her bag and stood up.

'Say goodbye to Wakana and the other girls from me.'

'I'll tell them if they turn up.'

Tokue opened the back door and stepped outside. Sentaro went with her, close by her side. Out on the street leaves drifted down from the cherry trees, hazily lit by streetlights.

'When I first came here the blossoms were out, but it's a sad sight now,' she said.

'The wind's cold, too.'

'I wonder if I'll see next year's blossom.'

'Of course you will. Tokue, please, will you come and teach me how to make bean paste again?'

Tokue smiled faintly but gave no answer.

'Thank you,' she said once more.

'I'm the one who should be thanking you. Truly, I mean it.'

Tokue put her hand out to stop Sentaro, who looked as if he was going to follow her. 'This is far enough,' she said.

He watched in silence as she walked off along the street into the night. The sight of her retreating back made Sentaro aware for the first time how physically small she actually was. Tokue was the one who'd brought up the topic of quitting. Sentaro had merely accepted her resignation, yet he felt as if he had driven his own mother away.

Pale-faced, he went back into the kitchen and stood there. His eyes fell on the bottle of alcohol disinfectant sitting on the edge of the counter, and he strode over to pick it up, then hurled it against the closed shutter.

15

Autumn advanced. Dead leaves gathered on the pavement outside the shop despite Sentaro's efforts at sweeping them up morning and night. People passed beneath the bare-branched cherry tree without stopping at Doraharu.

Sentaro surveyed this scene through bleary, hungover eyes. He was drinking more nowadays, going into the first bar he saw open after work, and although he never got violent, he would stay there clutching a glass until his legs became unsteady. In bed at night thoughts whirled about in his mind, words gnawed at his brain and he woke in the mornings with a heavy head.

After a while it got so bad that he could no longer arrive in time to make bean paste. Six o'clock became seven, then eight, and then nine. Some days he didn't leave for the shop until close to noon.

He felt as if everything on the street was rejecting him, even the cherry trees. The customers did not look like returning, and the very few regulars who still came had no reservations about voicing their complaints. 'I smelt something burning the other day,' one told him.

There were moments when Sentaro thought he should dispose of himself rather than the reject dorayaki pancakes. If he gave himself up to the moment, he might just be able to do it. At times he seriously considered this. But it wasn't just a question of what to do, he wanted nothing strongly enough to move him to action. He went through the days leadenly, moving only his eyes to peer out at the world.

The night when Wakana finally showed her face again, bare branches of the cherry tree bent in the wind. Sentaro had just turned off the griddle and was about to close up.

She wore a half-length coat and was clutching a bulky object wrapped in a green cloth that was so large it covered the top half of her body. She greeted Sentaro with a quick nod and placed the object on a counter seat.

'What's that?'

'Umm...'

'I'm closing up now.'

'Yeah,' Wakana muttered, but gave no sign of moving.

Sentaro took a dorayaki from the warmer and held it out to her. 'Don't just stand there, sit down,' he said.

'Thank you,' she replied softly. 'I guess Tokue's not here, is she?'

'No.'

Wakana looked at her dorayaki then turned back to Sentaro.

'What's up?' he asked her.

'Um, this is hard to say, but I don't have any money.'

'Huh?' Sentaro laughed. 'Don't worry. The shop's already closed for today.'

'Thank you.'

Wakana bowed slightly in thanks and took the dorayaki with both hands. Sentaro put another one on her plate.

'What's that?' he said, pointing to the object she had brought.

Wakana's hands stalled mid-air, just as she was about to take a bite of the dorayaki. She lowered her head. 'The thing is...'

'What?'

'The problem is...I, err, ran away from home.'

'Ran away?' Sentaro raised an eyebrow.

She nodded and reached over to the object next to her. 'This is a curtain,' she said and removed it to reveal a birdcage. A vivid splash of yellow moved inside.

'This baby has nowhere to go.'

'A canary?'

'His name's Marvy. I think he's a lemon canary. Anyway, he's why I came to see you.'

'This is why you ran away, is it? And you want me to...' Sentaro's voice trailed off, realizing he was about to be landed with another complicated problem.

'I promised Tokue.'

'Promised what?'

'Well...' Wakana hesitated and peered into the canary cage.

'Not the bird...'

'I think he was attacked by a cat or something. I found him about six months ago, flapping about on the side of the road all covered in blood. Marvy. I thought he'd die but I couldn't just leave him there, so I took him home and he got better. I put cream on his cuts every day, just did what I could, and he survived.'

'Well that's great.'

'But,' Wakana pointed to the cage, 'Marvy's a boy. So when he got better he started singing sometimes. That's the problem.'

'Why?'

'Because we live in a flat and can't keep pets. Mum kept telling me to let him go before the neighbour told the landlord. But Marvy can't fly very well 'cause his wings are stiff after his injuries. When I let him out of the cage inside, he just flies around a bit then flops on the floor. Mum's been on at me every day since summer to let him go. But the weather's getting colder and colder. Winter's coming and I don't think a canary could survive outside. Besides, he still can't fly well so a cat or a crow might get him again. How can I let him go knowing that?'

Sentaro filled a cup with water from the tap and took a sip. He grimaced as if it was sour.

'So, what's the favour?'

'Well I thought this might happen, so I asked

Tokue's advice before. Here.'

'Here?'

'Yes. When you took your mental-health break?'

'My mental-health break?'

'That's what Tokue said.'

The time he'd disappeared from the shop in early summer. Sentaro put his hand to his face. 'And what did Tokue say?'

'She said if I couldn't take care of him any more then you would.'

'Me?'

'Yes.'

The canary flapped its wings inside the cage and hopped around in a triangle. It gave a muffled chirp. Its voice was not like any canary Sentaro had heard before. Maybe this wasn't the season for singing.

'Tokue...How could she? Listen, sorry but I live in a flat too. I can't have pets either.'

'Tokue said that might happen. She said in that case maybe you could keep him here at the shop.'

'She really said that?'

'Yes.'

'How could she...?' Sentaro almost expressed his irritation in front of Wakana.

'I can't keep pets here. I'm not the owner, and besides, pets aren't usually allowed in places that serve food.'

'Really?'

'Yeah, can't do it.'

Wakana's face dropped. Disappointed, she looked at the bird in the cage.

'Wakana. Do you know why Tokue quit working here?'

Sentaro hesitated a moment. What exactly did he think he was going to say to a school girl? Now was the time to stop if he wasn't going to say any more. But he couldn't help himself. 'Wakana, remember you asked Tokue about her fingers?'

Wakana looked up from the canary and her eyes shifted uneasily from side to side. She nodded.

'She told you that she got sick when she was young, right?'

'Yeah.'

'Was that the first time you noticed her fingers, Wakana? Or had you seen them before?'

Wakana turned to look at Sentaro again. 'Before.'

'So why did you ask her that time?'

Cheep cheep, the canary sang.

'Because I thought it was better that way.' Her large misty eyes filled with a soft glow.

'Okay. In that case...Tokue was worried that sales at the shop had fallen. She said it might be her fault.'

'It's called Hansen's disease, isn't it?' Wakana asked.

Sentaro nodded. 'How did you know?'

'I told one person about her fingers.'

'Who?'

Wakana looked down at the dorayaki on her plate

then raised her face slowly.

'My mother.'

Wind blew through the door. Leaves driven by the wind knocked against the window with a dry papery sound.

'Aha. Your mother?'

'Yeah. And then she came here by herself one day.'

'And?'

'There's a Hansen's sanatorium near here, right? The bus goes all the way there. She said maybe it was someone from the sanatorium. So...she said I couldn't come here any more.'

The canary flew round in circles inside the narrow cage. Outside, leaves dropped from the cherry tree, one by one.

So that's what happened. Sentaro took his time to digest this, trying hard not to let the expression on his face change. The words came out anyway.

'Your mother. Do you think she told anybody about Tokue?'

'Dunno. But she works in a bar at night, so maybe she was drunk and told somebody. Some guy from round here p'raps.'

Wakana sat stiffly, staring into the kitchen.

'Your mother wasn't the only one,' Sentaro said softly. 'Other people certainly looked surprised when they saw Tokue's hands. I'm sure customers stopped coming because of it. Seems like rumours went around.'

'That's awful,' said Wakana, as if it had nothing to do with her.

Sentaro thought about how to respond. He made several false starts before he could get the words out. 'That's what public opinion is. That's why I can't let you leave that canary here. Everyone's afraid of bird flu these days. Ten years ago, maybe, but now people'd have a fit at the sight of a bird in a food and drink establishment.'

'I don't know.' Wakana stroked the wires of the birdcage with her fingertip. Marvy jumped in response. 'I think some people would come just because there is a canary around.'

Sentaro shook his head. 'It's not that simple.'

Wakana hung her head.

'But then...' Sentaro continued.

'What?'

'Well, I said public opinion like it's got nothing to do with me, but actually I did something much worse,' Sentaro confessed.

Wakana made no reply. She stroked the birdcage, and the canary hopped about inside, gently pecking near her finger. Eventually she pulled the finger away and looked askance at Sentaro.

'Because I didn't stand up for her when she said she was going to quit.'

'What do you mean?' Wakana asked.

'Even though she'd taught me how to make bean paste from scratch.'

There was a short silence.

'I don't really understand, but why don't you start over?' Wakana mumbled.

'Start over?'

'Yes.'

'What?'

'You're really worrying because of something else, aren't you?'

Sentaro made a noncommittal sound. This time it was his turn to hang his head.

'Have a go at starting over again.'

'It's not that easy...'

'Do you know her telephone number?' Wakana sat up straight.

Sentaro responded as if prodded. 'She doesn't have one apparently. But I know her address.'

'You know, that time I talked to Tokue, she said if you couldn't look after Marvy, then she would – as a last resort.'

'She said that? True?'

'She did. Honest. We were looking at the full moon together. You could see it above the cherry tree outside the shop. She said it was so lovely, we should go outside and look. Then while we were staring at the moon she said that about Marvy. It was a promise between the three of us – Tokue, and me, and the moon.'

'A promise to the moon? But I think Tokue lives in the sanatorium.'

'She said that though.'

'All right then, I'll write and ask.'

The light returned to Wakana's face. She turned the full weight of her dewy, shining eyes on Sentaro.

In the end he agreed to look after the canary until an answer came from Tokue. He took it back to his flat, praying that none of the neighbours would dob him in to the landlord.

16

A prickly holly hedge stretched as far as the eye could see.

Sentaro and Wakana found signs for the National Hansen's Disease Museum and Tenshoen National Sanatorium at the corner of a quiet suburban street leading off the busy main road and set off walking in that direction. The eastern side of the street was a residential area while the other side was bordered by an impenetrable holly hedge that extended into the distance like a green demarcating line without end. It reminded Sentaro of the place where he had once been shut up. They met nobody. The only sound in the air was birdsong.

Marvy chirped inside his cage as if in answer.

'This hedge goes on forever.'

'It's called false holly. See how the leaves are hard and spiky,' Wakana said.

'Holly like at Christmas.'

'Apparently they put this hedge all round to stop patients getting out.'

'But that was in the old days, right?'

'It's still here though, isn't it?' she responded.

Wakana had been doing some research on the internet too. She'd learned a bit about government policy on Hansen's disease patients and their forced segregation.

Sentaro brushed his fingertips on clusters of the hard, spiky leaves as they walked. The prickles hurt. He sensed that this was a far more forbidding barrier than the one he'd been imprisoned behind. Occasionally there were breaks in the hedge that presumably had once been passageways through it, but the trees grew dense and thick on the other side, obscuring any view into the grounds. They walked a long way, following the hedge, before the entrance to the National Hansen's Disease Museum finally came into view.

Around the museum the quietness was even more pronounced. Sunshine filtering through the trees dappled the ground outside the building. In the silence of shadows and light, the stillness was palpable.

Next to the museum entrance they saw a statue of a mother and daughter with the instantly recognizable hat, staff and garb of pilgrims. Which one was afflicted, wondered Sentaro, the mother or the daughter? In the past when one person caught the disease, the whole family – both parents and children – were forced to leave their homes to wander about in unfamiliar parts. Perhaps this statue was meant to console their spirits. Sentaro felt himself grow physically tense at the thought of all the pain and suffering this place represented.

They saw a sign in the car park with a map of the Tenshoen National Sanatorium grounds and searched for the shop, where they were to meet Tokue. It appeared to be more or less in the centre, next to the meeting hall and baths, and close to rows of orderly housing subdivisions with names such as 'Daybreak' and 'Venus'.

'We're early.'

Sentaro looked at his wristwatch. Wakana was right – there was still time before they were due to meet Tokue. 'Shall we walk around for a bit?'

'Yeah,' she responded.

Despite her affirmative reply Sentaro detected a note of reluctance in Wakana's voice. He recognized it because he felt the same. This had been an unknown world until very recently, one he had absolutely no connection with, but now here they were right inside it.

The Leprosy Prevention Act had been repealed in 1996. That year, former Hansen's patients became free at last to leave the sanatorium where they had been isolated from society. At the same time, town residents who previously had not been allowed to enter Tenshoen were permitted to pass through the gates. Nevertheless human lives had been swallowed up by this place and for a hundred years, continually spurned. It felt to Sentaro as if the singular silence rose from the very earth beneath their feet, steeped as it was in sighs and regrets.

They set off past the museum into the grounds following a path that was lined on both sides with imposing, tall cherry trees, now bare of leaves. These would be a magnificent sight in spring, Sentaro thought.

Still they saw nobody. Apart from birdsong they heard nothing.

'Sure is quiet here,' Sentaro remarked to fill the silence.

'Scary,' was how Wakana chose to express it.

They spotted a bench near the avenue of cherry trees and went over to sit down. Sentaro put the bird-cage on the ground and looked all about the deserted grounds: still no sign of human life. He saw orderly lines of single-storey row houses that made him think of a residential complex in a foreign country, or maybe army barracks – in any case, somewhere far removed from his life.

Silence engulfed them. A bicycle appeared in the distance, approaching from the other side of the cherry trees on a path that cut through the grounds. Since the grounds were open to anyone now, it could be a former patient still resident here, or someone from the neighbourhood.

The bicycle drew closer. They could see the rider was an elderly man who wore a hat with a brim. Sentaro suddenly wondered what his face looked like and hesitated – should he look at the man or not? Wakana looked down at the ground. Sentaro looked up and as the man passed by their eyes met. The cyclist's face was completely normal; he had a nose, and no obvious signs of paralysis. He, on the contrary, looked at Sentaro and

Wakana as if they were something unusual.

As the bicycle grew smaller in the distance, Sentaro asked himself what he thought he'd been doing, trying to examine the face of that man. He was about to go into the shop, a place where many of the people he would see might be former patients. Some of them might be severely disfigured – was he prepared for that? Then again, the fact that the word 'prepared' even came to mind probably meant he was wrong about himself: it wasn't his ability to control his reactions he was unsure of so much as his own deep-seated feelings.

'It's so quiet here I don't know what to make of it...'

'Because it's real? Because people really live here?' Wakana looked at the rows of housing.

'I guess so. This isn't like reading about something on the internet, it's for real,' said Sentaro.

Awed by the thought, they nodded at each other.

'Shall we head for the shop? It's a bit early, but Tokue is always early too.'

'Sure.'

They stood up and continued along the path indicated by the signboard. Thus far the avenue of trees had followed the contour of the boundary, but from here on they were heading deeper into the grounds, toward the shop.

The one-storey semi-detached buildings were divided into three or four units. Some had washing hanging out the front while others had tightly closed curtains.

It was still extremely quiet, with not even the sound of a distant TV or radio to break the silence. Then they heard a tinny melody like a music-box tune drifting through the air.

'Oh, look...' Wakana pointed to the other side of the houses, where a distinctive-looking truck was driving along the road very slowly. This was the source of the music. It gradually drew closer until it reached the road that they were now walking along, turned the corner and continued on ahead of them.

'What is it?' Wakana voiced the thought that was also in Sentaro's mind.

Three workers stood in the back of the truck, hanging onto a handrail. They were dressed from head to toe in white protective clothing. Sentaro and Wakana didn't know what the truck was for, but the sight of these workers riveted their eyes.

'Why do they have to wear that?' Wakana asked.

'Probably because this is a sanatorium – a hospital. I guess people are sensitive about germs here.' Sentaro blurted out the first thought that came to his mind.

'What about Marvy then?'

'You're right. A pet in a hospital might be—'

'But Tokue said it'd be okay.'

Sentaro glanced once more in the direction the truck had gone. If Hansen's disease was all but eradicated from Japan, what need was there for outlandish gear like that, he thought. No medical workers in the country had been infected through contact with patients. Why then didn't the workers here wear ordinary clothes? He began to feel anxious about having brought a young girl like Wakana here.

'Aha – people.' Wakana stopped.

They had passed the baths and chess hall, and she was looking at what looked like a co-op supermarket, which Sentaro guessed must be the shop. People stood around chatting outside.

'They're smiling,' Wakana said, looking straight at them.

All Sentaro's tension suddenly dissolved. His nervousness about meeting the residents dissipated the moment he saw them. They were just people. As Wakana said, they were laughing, and looked calm and relaxed.

One by one, Sentaro and Wakana passed by them as they approached the shop. They saw people with canes, and others holding bags of medicine in both hands. The man on the bicycle was there too. All appeared to be in varying degrees of health, but the one thing they had in common was their advanced age. One person turned and stared hard at Marvy inside his cage. In one group everybody seemed to be wearing sunglasses, perhaps because of some impediment.

'They're all the same age as Tokue,' Sentaro whispered to Wakana.

Then they were at the shop entrance. The door was wide open and they could see inside. It looked no different to any other supermarket. To the right were rows of shelves stocked with food and daily products. To their left was a drinks-vending machine near the wall and several round tables. Sitting alone, at a table next to the wall, was Tokue Yoshii.

17

Before Sentaro could say anything Tokue saw them and slowly rose from her seat. Her eyes darted from Sentaro to Wakana and back again. She blinked with one eye while holding her hands against her chest.

'Tokue.' Sentaro spoke first.

Tokue bobbed her head in greeting. 'Oh, it's been a long time since I saw your face,' she said. 'You, too, Wakana, dear.'

'I'm sorry it's been so long,' Sentaro answered.

'Yes, it has been a long time.' Tokue's face shone with happiness as she turned to Wakana, excitedly flapping her hands. 'Thank you for coming, both of you.'

'Not at all, we should be thanking you.' Sentaro held up the birdcage for her to see. 'Sorry to bother you with this.'

'What a beautiful yellow.'

'I think he's a lemon canary. He's called Marvy.' Wakana explained to Tokue how it had become impossible to keep Marvy at home after all. 'I didn't think he'd sing so much,' she said, her voice cracking with emotion.

'So now I'm looking after him, like I told you in the letter,' Sentaro added.

Tokue peered into the cage. 'Marvy,' she called to him.

'I wonder, though...is it really okay to have pets here?'

Tokue nodded. 'Oh, it's fine. I used to have a canary once.'

'Really?'

'Oh, thank goodness,' Wakana said.

Sentaro and Wakana were both greatly relieved to hear this.

'There are Neighbourhood Association rules. No dogs because they bark and are noisy, and once somebody got bitten by one. But a cat is okay, so small birds and animals are no problem. It's all right – I can take care of Marvy for you.'

'Thank you. That's a big help,' Sentaro said.

'Why were you worried anyway?' she asked.

'Well,' Sentaro hesitated, took a breath and went on. 'Because on our way here we saw a strange-looking truck. There were three workers standing in the back wearing some kind of protective clothing.' Sentaro looked at Wakana for confirmation.

'Yes,' Wakana continued. 'It looked like space suits.'

'So I thought maybe they have to wear that kind of gear because this is a hospital. And perhaps we shouldn't bring animals in here.'

Secretly, Sentaro was worried that people wore those clothes because there was still a possibility of infection, but of course he didn't mention that. It wasn't something he could very well say in front of Tokue.

'Oh, I know the truck you mean.' Tokue shook her head. 'It's not what you think. You must have wondered when you saw those outlandish suits. Yes, I can well understand. Nobody wears those suits here now, not workmen, or cleaners, or anyone working in the hospital. That truck was delivering food.'

'A food-delivery truck?' Wakana asked.

'Yes. It delivers meals. Breakfast, lunch and dinner for people who need it. So they wear the same kind of white uniform that people handling food in restaurants do. But now you mention it, I see what you mean. They're the only ones whose clothing hasn't changed since the old days.'

'So that's it.'

Sentaro and Wakana looked at each other.

'This place was established over a hundred years ago, but it's only recently a young girl like Wakana could enter these grounds freely. There's still a lot that needs changing.'

Only then did it occur to Sentaro that the people around them were all former Hansen's patients, and they might be able to hear this conversation. He wondered what they thought of him bringing up the topic of the food-delivery truck.

'It's all set, then. I'll take care of Marvy for you.'

'Thank you very much. We appreciate it,' Sentaro said with a low bow of thanks.

'It's all right, really.' Tokue smiled. 'I'm the one who's happy. My husband passed on ten years ago and I'm all alone, so it'll be good to have Marvy for company.'

'You were married? I didn't know.'

'Yes, I was. We never had children though.'

'But, you never...' Sentaro's voice trailed away as he realized where this might lead.

Tokue sensed his discomfort and went on. 'I married someone I met here. I'd already recovered, but it took a lot longer for my husband. Then he had a relapse...He had a hard life.'

'I'm sorry to hear it.'

There was nothing Sentaro and Wakana could do except listen and absorb Tokue's words.

'Talking about it even now...'

People sat at nearby tables drinking tea and coffee. Sentaro noticed them sneaking looks at himself and Wakana.

'But he put up a good fight,' Tokue continued.

'Did he die because of the relapse?'

'No, Hansen's disease isn't terminal. Even people with severe symptoms usually have a full lifespan. My husband had a bad heart. Just as we thought he was in the clear at last, he suddenly passed away.'

'Oh, I see.'

'But you know, even after death, people here can't

go back home to be buried. He was laid to rest in the charnel house here. I visit him every day.'

Cheep cheep, cried Marvy.

'He can sing,' said Tokue.

'Yes, he can,' Wakana told her. 'He loves to sing. But my mother said ordinary canaries' voices sound much better than he does.'

'When mating season comes it might improve,' Sentaro interposed.

Tokue laughed. 'It'd be a pity if he can't find a mate when it's time.' She brought her face up to the cage and mimicked a bird cheeping.

Wakana looked embarrassed. 'How about getting another bird then?' she mumbled.

'Yes, why not? A mate,' Tokue answered. 'What do I feed him? Bird food, and some lettuce and maybe some green leaves?'

'Yes. He needs vegetables.'

'He's got a good appetite, this one,' Sentaro added.

'Oh dear, excuse me.' Tokue's nose had dripped as she leaned over the cage. She pulled a packet of tissues from her pocket. 'I've got a bit of a cold that's been hanging on for a while.'

'Well that's understandable. You were tired out by the time you finished up at Doraharu.'

'Yes, I was. I haven't been quite myself since then.' Tokue blew her nose. 'Pardon me,' she muttered softly. 'In the old days this would never be forgiven. People used to believe the sickness was spread through nasal

111

mucus. That wasn't entirely wrong, though.'

She opened the neck of a drawstring bag and delicately dropped her tissue inside.

Wakana followed her movement out of the corner of her eye. 'When did you first come here?' she asked abruptly.

Sentaro tried to interrupt but Tokue didn't bat an eyelid. 'When I was about your age,' she said to Wakana.

'My age?'

'Yes. I lived way out in the countryside when I was a child. After Japan lost the war, times were very hard. My elder brother came back from the war in China so thin he looked like a ghost, and there wasn't enough for the whole family to eat. In the middle of all that my father died. Of pneumonia.'

'Didn't you have medicine?' Wakana spoke in a low voice.

Tokue shook her head and smiled wryly. 'Not in those days.'

Cheep cheep, cried Marvy.

Chatter from surrounding tables rose and fell in waves. Sentaro and Wakana drew closer to Tokue to hear her.

'Eventually my two older brothers found work. My younger sister and I did farm work. Just as we were starting to think we'd get by somehow...out of the blue...I never thought...One day I noticed a red lump on my thigh.' She pointed to her right leg.

'For a long time I wondered what it was. My mother worried too and took me to see a doctor in the next town, but he didn't know. He just gave me some medicine to take. After a while it looked like it was spreading. And I was losing feeling in the sole of my foot. When I pinched it, I didn't feel any pain. I was starting to think it was all very strange, when the doctor called me back, and my mother and elder brother went with me.'

Marvy had become accustomed to the surroundings by now, and burst into loud song. People from other tables wandered over to look at him. Tokue stopped talking and waited for them to finish commenting on the canary.

'The doctor ordered me to come here, to Tenshoen,' she continued. 'I wasn't told anything but my mother and brother seemed to know what was happening. You can't imagine what an enormous thing it was in those days to make a journey from home, deep in the country, to the edge of Tokyo. We went home and that night my mother cooked up a special meal using anything she could find. We had fried egg, which was a real luxury then. My sister was over the moon about that at first, but then she started to get sad because my mother was crying. My brother told everyone I might have a serious sickness that was difficult to treat and wouldn't come home for a while, so we should all be prepared. I did my best to smile and eat everything, but of course I couldn't get anything down after hearing that.'

'Didn't they tell you what was wrong?' Sentaro asked.

'Uh, well...' Tokue made vague noises, 'not directly. I never expected this, and didn't want to believe it might be anything like it. But then next day I had to leave with my oldest brother.'

'What about your mother?' Wakana asked.

'She came as far as the station. She cried and apologized to me. She'd stayed up late to make me a new blouse from a white knit fabric. I wondered where she found the material. It was a long time since – or maybe even the first time – I'd worn anything like it. When I thought about being away from my family, I was so lonely and scared. I wore that blouse at the station and hugged my mother goodbye. We both cried. My other brother and sister didn't come to the station – they said goodbye to me at the front door, for the last time. My sister couldn't stop crying. I was crying too, but I kept telling her it's okay, I'll come back. Then I got on the train for the long journey to Tokyo. It took all night to get here, and when we got off my brother finally told me on the platform that I might have leprosy. If it turned out I did, he was going to have to leave me here—'

Tokue broke off. She looked down at the table and slowly closed her eyes. Then she dug out another tissue with her crooked fingers and gently pressed it to her eyes and nose.

'How old were you then, Tokue?' Sentaro asked.

Tokue paused. 'Fourteen,' she said finally, then loudly blew her nose. 'I underwent an examination and afterwards had to get in a disinfectant bath. They disposed of everything I wore or brought with me. I begged the nurse in tears to let me keep the blouse my mother made. But she said no, that was the rule. I asked her to give it to my brother at least so he could take it back with him. Then she told me he'd already gone, that I didn't have family with me any more. And she said I should use a different name from now on. That's what they said...that's what we were told to do...I cried and screamed at the top of my voice – why did this have to happen to me? I knew what would happen. People with leprosy weren't allowed out in society. I'd seen lepers before and thought they were scary. But never once did I ever imagine that would be me...' Tokue faltered again.

'What about the blouse?' Sentaro asked gently.

'I never saw it again. The blouse my mother made disappeared forever. I was given two striped cotton kimonos instead – that's all patients were allowed. They told me I wouldn't get any new ones for two years, so I should take good care of them. I was just a girl...'

'Toku, Toku.' A soft voice came from behind them.

Tokue looked up. 'Ah,' she said, and waved.

'Toku dear, it's okay. I'll just leave this here and be off.'

Sentaro and Wakana turned to look in the direction of the voice. They saw an elderly woman whose face was markedly disfigured – much more severely than Tokue's – and whose lower lip hung down to reveal her gums.

Sentaro didn't know how to react. He and Wakana simply nodded a greeting.

'My name's Moriyama. Toku and I've been making sweets together all these years.'

'I, err...Tokue has been a great help to me.'

'You must be the dorayaki man?'

'Yes, that's me.'

'I wish I could've worked there too.' With this she placed a plastic bag on the table and said, 'I'll be running along,' then smiled and left the shop.

Sentaro and Wakana could see the bag contained something wrapped in aluminium foil.

'If it doesn't bother you, why don't you open it up and have a look?' said Tokue. 'Miss Moriyama must've been baking.'

If he were honest, Sentaro did not feel like putting anything from that bag into his mouth. He was still shaken by Tokue's story, and slightly shocked from seeing someone severely disfigured by Hansen's disease close-up for the first time. Tokue, sensing Sentaro's state of mind, reached for the bag and lifted out the foil packet. She opened it up and took out a wafer-thin biscuit.

'Mm, *tuile*!'

'Twill?' said Sentaro.

'A French biscuit, very thin and crispy,' Tokue replied, holding one out each to Sentaro and Wakana.

'It's got almond and orange in it. Very easy to make.'

'You seem to know a lot. My business is confectionery but I had no clue...'

Sentaro took the biscuit and brought it to his mouth. It would be a lie to say he felt no hesitation, but the moment it touched his lips the rich citrus aroma dispelled all doubt. The aroma intensified once he bit into a sliver of almond.

'Mm, this is interesting,' he said.

'Isn't it? It smells just like cooked fruit,' Wakana sounded brighter too. She broke fragments of the *tuile* off with her fingers and put them in her mouth.

'How did you come to know about a biscuit like this? If you and the other lady have been in here all this time?'

Tokue made a noncommittal sound and folded the packet of *tuile* up.

'Let's go for a little walk, shall we?' she suggested, and they all stood up to leave.

18

The three set out on the road through the grounds, with Sentaro carrying Marvy's cage. Away from the shop, the quietness returned.

'For treatment – such as it was – we didn't have drugs like Promin at first.'

Promin: this was the name of the drug used for treating Hansen's disease. Sentaro and Wakana both knew from their reading on the internet the change it brought about in ending a long history of suffering.

'But that medicine helped cure you, didn't it?' Wakana asked, standing close by Tokue's side.

'We'd all heard about it, and how incredibly effective it was. But it wasn't getting to Japan. That's why we patients banded together to get action, and started a campaign to let us have access to Promin. There were protests in every sanatorium. Any earlier and we would have been thrown in detention cells for that.

'Detention cells? You had that kind of thing? I—' Sentaro broke off in confusion before he could let slip anything about his own experience of cells.

'The Kusatsu sanatorium had a solitary cell. Every sanatorium had detention cells, but if anyone got sent to isolation in Kusatsu there was little chance of coming back alive. People were locked up for months at a time in a pitch-black room with no sun. In winter it was sealed off by snow and they'd freeze to death.'

Wakana's face registered shock.

'People go crazy in the dark and die,' Tokue said gently. 'People from here got sent to detention in Kusatsu, too, for starting a strike, and died there.'

What must Tokue have seen here as a young girl, Sentaro wondered, with thoughts of his own time behind bars. What must she have gone through?

'If I hadn't gotten sick, though, I wouldn't have given another thought to what happened to people with this disease. When I was little I saw tramps taken away on police trucks because they were suspected of having leprosy. Public-health workers came and squirted them down mercilessly with white powder while they crouched down in the back. Because I'd seen that kind of thing, I was scared of lepers. For a long time after I came here, it was unbearable to have to see them every day. Even if I was one.'

Sentaro wanted to say something sympathetic, but words failed him.

'The ones that got brought here after their illness was far gone had symptoms all over their bodies,' Tokue continued in a subdued tone. 'There were people with nodules, big lumps and scabs – that's the kind of thing this illness does to you. Some had their fingers fall off, others their nose. It wasn't an unusual sight

119

before the medicine became available. It was dreadful seeing people suffering like that, knowing that's what would happen to me eventually. I was terrified.'

Tokue stopped walking. They had reached a lone small hillock that looked almost man-made. Late-autumn grass blooms dotted the slope among the trees and shrubs.

'We all longed for home. This is where we came when we felt homesick.' Tokue pointed to steps cut into the earth and leading up the slope.

'This hill was here before I arrived. Able-bodied patients built it from earth they dug up when they were forced to clear the forest. People would climb up to see the mountains in the distance and think about where they came from.'

'Did you used to climb up here too, Tokue?' Wakana asked.

Tokue stood still. She made no move to lead them up the steps.

'Yes I did. Many times. But all it did was make me feel sad, because I couldn't go outside. Downright miserable, in fact. So I stopped coming here. Instead—' She broke off and sneezed loudly once, then pulled out the tissues again to blow her nose. 'The colds going around this year are quite stubborn.' Tokue suddenly smiled. 'That was an order from himself, warning me not to speak badly of him.'

Sentaro looked at Tokue quizzically.

'My husband,' she answered. 'The last time I was

up there, I was having a little cry by myself when somebody spoke to me. The man who became my husband.'

'Really? What was he like?' Wakana asked.

Tokue laughed. 'What can I say? I still don't know,' she said bewilderingly.

They set off again along a path leading out of the dense woods. Thick layers of leaf litter covered the ground. Sentaro felt more like they were walking through ancient forest than the grounds of a sanatorium.

Sentaro and Wakana walked behind Tokue in silence.

Abruptly she began speaking again, as if she had just remembered something. 'Of course he couldn't go off to the war because he was born with a weak heart. But he worked. Can you guess what he did?'

Sentaro shook his head.

'He worked at a confectioner's in Yokohama.'

'Really? Then...'

'Yes. I learned everything I know about confectionery from my husband.'

'So that's how you learned,' replied Sentaro, sounding brighter than he had since setting foot in the grounds of Tenshoen.

'Now I get it,' said Wakana beside him.

'He was a tall man – like a palm tree. After he found out he was sick and quit his job at the confectioner's, he decided to die on the road. He travelled around the whole of Japan like a beggar. But he'd have been better off coming straight to the sanatorium instead.'

'I bet he wanted to escape all this,' said Wakana.

Tokue looked at Wakana with a pained expression. 'Yes, I'm sure he did. You're probably right. By the time he was brought here the disease had progressed a lot. He was always tossing and turning about because of the pain. I couldn't bear to watch him. The nerve inflammation was so bad it made holes in his hands. But you know, I rarely ever heard him speak bitterly or curse the gods. That man had great powers of endurance.'

'Why...Why did something like that happen to him?'

'What do you mean?' Sentaro asked Wakana, with his eyes still on Tokue.

'Why is it that a simple confectionery-maker has to suffer so much?'

'Isn't that the truth,' Tokue said, walking slowly ahead of them. 'Isn't it indeed...' she said again. 'Anyone who was ever shut up in here has thought that. I'd like to get hold of the gods – if there really are any – and give them a good clout for all they put us through.'

'You've been through a lot,' Sentaro said.

Tokue nodded emphatically. 'But you know, we just tried to get on with our lives as best we could.'

She stopped walking. Sentaro and Wakana halted too.

'In the old days, the fire truck wouldn't come here if there was a fire. Police wouldn't come if there was a crime. That's how isolated we were. We had to do everything for ourselves. We formed our own neighbourhood associations and even made our own money. We had currency you couldn't use anywhere except here.'

'Even money?' Wakana's mouth fell open.

Tokue nodded. 'That's right,' she said. 'There was no choice. We all had to pull together to get by. There was a woman who used to be a geisha before she got sick, she made kimonos and taught traditional ballad singing. A former teacher ran the school for children. A barber cut people's hair. That's how we did everything. We had Western needlework and Japanese-style needlework groups, as well as a gardening group and a fire-fighting squad.

Tokue walked off slowly again. Tiny flowers on the side of the path quivered in the breeze. This could be a beautiful woodland scene anywhere, thought Sentaro.

'Everybody had experience of some kind in society. As that geisha used to say, everyone has their own talent. That's why my husband and I had no hesitation about joining a particular work group.'

Tokue looked back, her head framed by the delicate wildflowers in the background. Sentaro and Wakana were following behind her, and stopped when she did.

'We joined the Confectionery Group.'

'There was such a thing?' Sentaro said.

'Yes, there was. Had been for a long time apparently.

In the beginning it was just people who got together to make pounded rice at New Year and *kusamochi* pounded-rice cakes with mugwort and sweet bean paste in the spring. I guess it was started by a professional confectionery-maker who came here in the past.'

'So that's why you were making sweet bean paste the last fifty years!' Sentaro clapped his hands. At last the mystery was solved.

'We didn't just make bean paste, you know. We did Western-style confectionery as well.'

'And that's why you thought of putting cream in a dorayaki,' said Wakana excitedly.

'That's right.' Tokue smiled.

'The Tenshoen Confectionery Group...' Sentaro repeated.

'Yes, it's been going a long time. We had to do something to make life better. With this disease the eyesight gets weaker and sensation in the fingers and toes is gradually lost. But for some reason sensation in the tongue is the last to be affected. Can you imagine what it's like for someone who can't see or feel, to taste something sweet?'

Sentaro drew a long breath. He didn't know what to say.

'Wow,' said Wakana, and fell silent.

'You've had a hard time,' said Sentaro, recovering himself.

Tokue mumbled something indistinctly. 'The one who really had a hard time is in there,' she said with a faint smile, pointing her crooked fingers along the path to where it ended and woodlands gave way to bushes.

They saw a stone tower looming over a clipped grassy area.

'That's where my husband was laid to rest,' Tokue said as she approached the tower with slow, deliberate steps.

'In the old days, if it got out that someone had leprosy, the rest of the family had to leave their home too. That's how strong fears about it were. It's also why most of us had our names struck from the official family registers, and never got them restored. Tokue Yoshii is the name I was given when I came here.'

'What?' Sentaro stared at Tokue. 'It's not your real name?'

Wakana, too, was wide-eyed in disbelief.

'That's right. It's not my real name.'

'Really...I can't believe...' Sentaro couldn't finish the sentence and fell silent. Wakana said nothing.

They reached the stone cairn and stopped in front of it.

'This is the charnel house for those who die at Tenshoen.'

'What's a charnel house?' Wakana asked.

'A place to put bones. We don't have graves. My husband, Yoshiaki, is here too. Free from pain at last. I'm sure he's dreaming of his favourite bean-jam buns.'

Tokue put her hands together. 'Yoshiaki, I brought some young people with me today.'

Sentaro watched her small frame from behind. He

put the birdcage down and joined Wakana as they put their hands together in prayer.

A bulbul sang a long melodic warble and Marvy twittered in reply.

'I, um...' Tokue dropped her hands. 'When the day came we were finally allowed to leave this place, I thought I could return home. But it was difficult. My mother and brothers were dead by then. I got in contact with my sister but...she begged me not to go back, so I couldn't. I had nowhere to go back to. Yoshiaki didn't have any family who'd take him back either. The bones of more than 4,000 people are in here. When the law changed, for one happy moment we all thought we could go home. But more than a dozen years have passed since then and almost no one has come forward to take us back. The world hasn't changed. It's just as cruel as it always was.'

Tokue spoke flatly, as if talking about someone else. Then she turned to Wakana and smiled. 'Sorry to burden you with so much sadness today, my dear. But I tell you, it's a weight off my chest to be able to talk about it. Thank you for listening.'

Wakana shook her head quickly side to side as if to say, not at all. 'Tell me more if you like,' she said.

'You too, boss,' said Tokue, turning to Sentaro. 'Thank you.'

'Not at all, really. You're doing us a favour taking the canary. Besides...I want to ask your advice about something. May I come again?'

Tokue looked at Sentaro and nodded. 'I'd like that, but...' Her voice trailed off with an unspoken thought.

A wide path led them away from the charnel house. In the distance they could see the outline of the shop and a building that might have been the bathhouse. They could have come directly on this path, but Tokue had chosen to take them on the longer, more indirect route through the woods.

As they were heading back through the centre of the park again, Sentaro felt a tugging sensation at his back. He turned around and saw the stone cairn at the charnel house.

Four thousand souls. Four thousand people who never went home. He felt their eyes boring down on him from above.

19

That night Sentaro went to bed without a drop to drink. He felt shivery and feverish. Lying curled up under the covers, he went over the day at Tenshoen in his mind like a clock turning backwards.

He saw images of the charnel house shining in the evening sun, the path through the woods, flowers in bloom at the path's edge, the hillock built by patients to remember their hometowns, the woman who'd brought them the biscuits...Then he suddenly remembered Tokue blowing her nose.

Hansen's was transmitted by nasal mucus...Tokue had said that.

A chill swept through his burning body and he squirmed. Why, he wondered. Tokue had been cured more than forty years ago. So long ago you almost hesitated to use the term former patient. Why did he feel this way when he should know better than anyone? Sentaro could not understand where his anxiety sprang from.

Was Wakana all right? He fervently hoped she was not sick too. Sentaro put his hand on his forehead and felt the burning heat. He recalled Wakana keeping her face down and averted the whole time on their way back. They were both shaken by the day's experience.

After saying goodbye to Tokue they had visited the National Hansen's Disease Museum next to Tenshoen and walked through its wide spaces barely exchanging a word. They encountered a world, new to both of them, of unfathomable grief and suffering, that had long been buried in darkness. Sentaro was glad they had visited, he wouldn't have wished otherwise. Although he could not put it into words precisely, he felt he had gained something from seeing and hearing the testimony of people who had lived through such adversity. At the same time his brain reeled with the images he had seen that now would not go away, whether his eyes were open or closed. Like the photograph entitled 'Tongue Reading' of an elderly patient who was so severely affected by the disease it had robbed him of his sight and the nerve-endings in his fingers and toes. As a result the man was unable to sense Braille bumps with his numb fingertips. But for some reason sensation in the tongue was the last to be lost, so instead of his fingertips he used the tip of his tongue to read, tracing each character one by one. The image of the straight-backed old man licking a book with his tongue was burned into his mind's eye.

There were numerous such photos. In one, a group of men made music with fingerless hands wrapped around harmonicas, and in another, an elderly woman was completely absorbed in making pottery with bent, gnarled hands.

Sentaro had no connection to these people before now, but for some reason they had gotten inside him, whispering things in his ear and looking at him with troubled expressions. Sentaro couldn't bear it and doubled over. His breath came out in feverish gasps.

He thought about the path they had taken through the woods today. How many of them had walked along it hidden by those trees? And what about that prickly hedge ferociously shutting out the world? What did they feel when they saw it? He supposed it was an entirely different emotion from the sense of defeat he used to feel when he was behind bars. He'd been in the wrong – these people were innocent. There was a limit to his confinement – but when they had entered the law ordained they would be there for the rest of their lives.

If it had been him, what would he have felt and thought as he walked around those grounds? Would he have felt deep anger? Or then again, perhaps he would have done his best to forget about the world outside.

Absorbed in these thoughts, Sentaro drifted off into a feverish doze. Suddenly he noticed that he seemed to have returned to the path and was walking along it again, heading over towards where the trees were thick. He went a little further and came to a clearing of cut grass. On the edge of the clearing a young girl stood wearing a rough cotton kimono.

Sentaro knew immediately who she was; a four-teen-year-old girl who had been brought here, not understanding why; the young Tokue, who wept and wept until she had no more tears to shed.

Sentaro stood behind her trying to think of words of comfort. But he knew that there was nothing he could say that would be of any help.

What must she be feeling, this young girl, after being told she could never go out into the world beyond that hedge again, and knowing that her face might become disfigured. Where would she find hope?

Sentaro stood staring at her back.

What were the forces that played with this life? If she were being toyed with out of spite, at some point it would end, and she could move on. For example if public opinion were against her, times change, and eventually she could walk in the sun again one day. But who or what would want to torment a girl of only fourteen for the rest of her life?

The thought was oppressive.

Of course...it had to be the gods who were behind it all. The gods who whispered in her ear that she was better off not being born. The gods who declared she must suffer her whole life. What did Tokue think about life once she understood this? How was she going to live out the rest of it?

She was just a girl, quietly sobbing her heart out.

Sentaro could watch no more. He turned and went back along the forest path.

20

A cold autumn wind blew, shaking the few remaining leaves from the cherry tree outside Doraharu. People on the street were wrapped up in coats and scarves.

Inside and out the cold was bone-chilling. Over a month had passed since Tokue departed, and the end of the year approached. Sales had not improved. The owner had taken to dropping by frequently and muttering comments about not making it through the year as she stared at the books.

In spite of everything, Sentaro's sweet bean paste showed signs of improving. A number of customers had remarked on how much better it was. He had cut back on drinking and was getting up early again to make the bean paste. Recently, as he stood over the copper pot every day, Sentaro consciously tried to emulate Tokue's methods: he divided up the time and regulated the heat and water much as she had. There were days when he sensed he might be a little bit closer to her standard.

But the world was not such a forgiving place that this meant a recovery in sales. In business it was understood that customers who leave – for whatever reason – don't come back. Sentaro was experiencing this first-hand. Even the owner was saying they might as well be done with dorayaki and start selling *okonomiyaki* savoury pancakes or some such thing instead. Not so long ago Sentaro would have agreed with her; now he did his best to politely fend off her suggestions. For the last few years all he had wanted was to escape the grind of this work – standing over a hot griddle every day – but now he could not bring himself to agree to close down Doraharu. He didn't really understand the reason why. All he knew was how strongly he felt about not wanting the shop to close.

The day the letter arrived a cold rain had been falling since morning. Sentaro looked up after he finished making the bean paste to notice it poking out of the letterbox. The envelope was addressed in a familiar handwriting to Sentaro Tsujii, care of Doraharu.

Dear Sentaro,

How are you? I hope you are well. The weather has turned very cold and wintry, hasn't it? I'm still trying to shake off this cold, and am in and out of bed with it.

How are things at Doraharu? After seeing you I had a feeling that it might be getting you down, so I was a bit worried. I still think of you and the shop.

Remember how you always used to ask me what I was doing while I was making the bean paste? I used to put my face up close to the adzuki and you'd ask if I could hear anything. Well, Listening was the only answer I had, but I thought if I said that it'd confuse you, so I didn't explain.

One thing I can do in Tenshoen is sniff the wind and listen to the murmur of the trees. I pay attention to the language of things in this world that don't use words. That's what I call Listening, and I've been doing it for sixty years now.

When I make sweet bean paste I observe closely the colour of the adzuki beans' faces. I take in their voices. That might mean imagining a rainy day or the beautiful fine weather that they have witnessed. I listen to their stories of the winds that blew on their journey to me.

It's my belief that everything in this world has its own language. We have the ability to open up our ears and minds to anything and everything. That could be someone walking down the street, or it could be the sunshine or the wind. I realize I may have seemed like a nagging old woman to you, and I regret that for all I said I couldn't pass this vital message on to you.

When I walk through the woods at Tenshoen I think of Doraharu, you, those sweet young girls, and Wakana. Ever since I became estranged from my sister I don't know anyone else living out in the world. Now that I'm not sure how much longer I have left, I feel as if you and Wakana are my family.

Maybe that's why, when I thought about you, I heard whispers in the wind that blew from the other side of the hedge, and I felt in my bones it might be a good idea to contact you.

I suppose that rumours must have spread about me, and you are probably still having a hard time as a result. If that's the case, I made a mistake in not quitting sooner than I did. I try to live a blameless life, but am crushed at times by peoples' lack of understanding. Sometimes you just have to use your wits. That's something else I should have told you.

But now, you and I both have to get over this. It's sad, but it can't be helped. Please take pride in yourself as a professional confectioner and do the best you can to get through this.

In any case, I feel sure that you are capable of creating your own dorayaki. I've been making sweet bean paste for a long time but that doesn't mean you have to do everything the way I do. It's important to be bold and decisive. When you can say with certainty that you have found your style of dorayaki, that will be the start of a new day for you. I firmly believe this. Please have the courage to go your own way. I know that you can do it.

Yours sincerely,

Tokue Yoshii

P.S. Marvy is doing well. He loves green-leaf vegetables and eats a lettuce leaf every day. The only thing that worries me is he's started saying that he wants to go outside. I don't know what that's all about. Please come and see me again with Wakana. Let's talk about it then.

Sentaro read the letter over and over again. He even forgot to turn the griddle on. Tokue's voice echoed from each character written in that distinctive wavy handwriting. He felt as if she were standing right there, speaking to him.

Since there were no customers in sight, Sentaro ran to the convenience shop to buy writing paper.

Dear Tokue,

Thank you for taking the trouble to write when you are still not well. I read your letter here in the shop many times. I don't remember feeling so heartened in a long time.

'Listening' is a good word. I like it. Now I know what you were doing when you had your face up so close to the beans. You were looking at each one, and drawing on fifty years of experience to bring out the potential of every single bean. I knew you were looking at them carefully, but I thought you were only concerned with getting the heat right, and rinsing the right number of times to remove bitterness, things like that. I never dreamed you were listening to them whisper about where they were born and brought up.

137

If anyone else but you had told me this I would not believe it. Mostly because I've never actually listened to language in the way you describe. But then I didn't even listen to my own mother, which is something I never spoke of before.

There was a time when I couldn't go out into the world either, but for a very different reason than you. As a rule, I don't tell people about it, but I think it'd be good to tell you now. A few years before I started working at Doraharu I broke the law for no particular reason. I went to jail as a result and spent time looking up at a small patch of sky.

My mother came to see me several times. But we never exchanged more than two or three words. She passed away before I got out. By the time my father found her she was already dead, of a stroke.

Of course I said the necessary apologies to my mother, but that was all. We weren't speaking much at the time so I couldn't tell her anything or hear what she had to say. The thought of that is painful even now. It weighs heavily on me. I gave up on my own mother and I'm still a failure. Sorry to go on so much about myself, but this is who I am.

However, after spending all that time making bean paste with you, I feel like I might have changed a little. Up to now all I could think about was paying off my debts so I could leave Doraharu, but now I feel attached to the place. You're the one who brought about that change in me. That's why I believe in you and your sense of things. I still can't feel it myself, but I like the idea that everything has its own language, and that we can be sensitive to it.

The fight at Doraharu still continues. A few customers have good things to say about my bean paste, but I'm still a long way off being able to pull in customers with it. To tell the truth, I'm in a very bad position right now. I'm afraid the wind might have blown word of my worries in your direction.

The other day when we came to see you I had another favour I wanted to ask you besides the canary. But I was so overwhelmed by everything I heard and saw that I couldn't bring it up.

I know it's selfish of me to mention this when I ought to be worried about your health, but I still need you to teach me something. I can more or less make sweet bean paste now by copying what you do. But when it comes to going beyond that and making my own kind of dorayaki, I have no idea what to do or what direction to take. If I could make my own style of dorayaki, like you said, maybe a time will come when customers start lining up again. It would save Doraharu and would be a new start for me too.

The other thing is, I'd really like to learn more from you about confectionery in general. I have a feeling that if I could, some things might become clearer to me. Can I please come and visit you again at Tenshoen?

I'll also have a chat with Wakana about the canary. She's in her last year of middle school at the moment though, and might be busy with exams coming up. I can't make any promises right now about when we can come to see you together, but I will make the time to come by myself. I hope to talk with you about a lot of things when I do.

Well, I'll stop here. I'm sorry this letter is all about my troubles and failings.

The weather is getting much colder now, so I hope you will take good care of yourself and not let your cold get any worse.

Yours sincerely,

Sentaro Tsujii

21

The new year arrived, bringing rain mingled with snow. Not once did the sun show its face for three days straight.

Sentaro kept the shop open nevertheless. There seemed no point in drinking festive spiced sake alone so instead he set to work making bean paste in the dark of early morning and opened up the shop earlier than usual. He thought he might be able to sell to people making their way to the other side of the station in order to pay the traditional shrine visit during the New Year period.

Yet sales were poor, as he feared they might be. When the owner came to check the books very early in the new year, she sighed pointedly and muttered again about turning Doraharu into another kind of food shop. An *okonomiyaki* shop might have been just a spur-of-the-moment thought when she first brought it up, but increasingly she seemed genuinely taken with the idea and asked Sentaro if he would still work for her if she did that. Sentaro gave no sign of agreement.

'Let's give dorayaki a go for a bit longer,' he told her. 'After all, the boss started this shop – we should respect his memory. Besides, I still have a debt left to pay.'

She nodded ambiguously and pursed her lips. 'If you want to stay in business it doesn't matter what you sell. We all have to make a living.'

Sentaro recognized there was some truth in that, but still could not agree. It was business, too, to commit to providing a certain standard of bean paste, even if it didn't go well. He didn't feel that a business – of any kind – should be run with an anything-goes kind of attitude.

And there was something else too, something far more important to Sentaro: Tokue's sweet bean paste. He was determined to carry on making it, because if he did not, it would disappear from the world. Apart from its merits as a bean paste, Sentaro thought of it as testimony to the life of a remarkable woman called Tokue Yoshii.

In mid-January Sentaro received a winter greeting card from Tokue, the same day he had an argument with the owner about the future of Doraharu. Dorayaki didn't seem to exist in her mind any more. As usual Sentaro maintained that they should be patient a little longer but could not explain his basis for saying that.

Naturally he was frustrated too. When he thought of all the customers who never came any more he felt like cursing them. But seeing Tokue's handwriting on the postcard again made him feel slightly better. She wrote that she had been ill and in bed over the new year period, and she apologized for not sending a New

Year greeting card, and finished up by saying that she was better and asked if he would like to visit again. 'When you do, I'll revive the Confectionery Group with Miss Moriyama,' she wrote.

'I'll go,' Sentaro said to himself when he read this, standing alone in the kitchen. 'I don't have many customers anyway.'

Tenshoen was as quiet as ever. With the trees now bare of leaves, the stillness seemed to penetrate even more keenly. A biting cold wind blew through the grounds beneath a clear, sunny sky.

He followed the same route as last time to the shop where he was to meet Tokue. The deserted path was cloaked in silence; he met nobody along the way. Reaching the shop, he passed through entrance and his feet stopped. 'Tokue...' He was shocked by the alteration in her appearance.

Miss Moriyama, who had given them the *tuile* on his previous visit, was by her side.

'Hello,' he said as he approached the table, 'it's been a while.'

Sentaro was shocked by Tokue's appearance and tried not to let his agitation show. Though it was only just over a month since they had last met, she looked as if years had passed. She returned his smile readily, but her eyes were hollow and her cheeks sunken.

'Tokue, you've had a rough trot with that cold, it seems.'

'Yes, I have. It's been hard going. I couldn't eat...'
She ran her fingers through her tousled white hair that
stood up in waves like the bark of a palm tree.

'She was very poorly for a while. At one stage I
thought I'd have to call you.'

Miss Moriyama contorted her own disfigured face
into something resembling Munch's *Scream*, to illus-
trate how gaunt Tokue had been.

'Oh, get on with you. I'm better now.'

'Sorry. But I thought you were going off after your
husband for a while there.'

'Not for a while yet. I have to finish teaching the
boss here how to make the Confectionery Group's
sweet bean paste.'

Despite her gauntness, Tokue's voice had a surprisingly bright spring in it.

'Are you really all right?' Sentaro said, peering at
Tokue's face.

She waved her hand as if to shield herself from his
searching gaze. 'I'm better now. But it was hard over
New Year, so I kept to my bed.'

'I'm sorry I didn't realize earlier,' he said.

'Oh, don't worry about that. I'm just glad you're
here now.'

Miss Moriyama stood up and left the table, giving them a few moments alone. She came back a short
while later holding a tray with both hands. 'Here we
are,' she said, putting the tray down. On it were three
bowls with steam gently rising from them.

145

'I heated it up on the stove out the back.'

Sentaro looked in the bowl. 'Oh, this is...'

'We're doing a rerun of New Year,' said Tokue, putting her hands together in a gesture of thanks for the food.

'It's sweet bean soup, the Confectionery Group's specialty.' Miss Moriyama sounded cheery, too.

The sweet bean paste that Sentaro knew so well glistened inside the bowls, each sparkling bean bound to all the others in a thick soup. The rich, sweet aroma wafted over to nearby seats.

'Mm, smells good,' came a voice from another table.

'Please, start.' Miss Moriyama placed a bowl in front of Sentaro.

'Eat while it's hot. I think you'll find it to your taste even if you don't have a sweet tooth,' Tokue encouraged him.

Sentaro had never actually managed to consume a whole bowl of this traditional sweet New Year's dish before, but after the first mouthful, his face relaxed.

'This is really good!' The words tumbled out spontaneously. The sweetness seemed to melt away the tension in his cheeks and neck, and was followed quickly by a feeling of relief.

'Toku, dear. Don't forget the rest,' Miss Moriyama said.

'Oh yes, that's right. Sentaro, try this as well.' Tokue took a small plastic container from her bag and tipped the contents into a dish.

'This is good. It's Toku's special homemade salty *kombu*.'

'Salty *kombu*?'

'It's not the same without it,' said Miss Moriyama, taking a pinch of the *kombu*. 'Mm, perfect,' she said, nodding to herself.

Sentaro also reached for a piece. It was cut into strips of just the right size in length and width, and gave off a pleasant plum scent that tickled the back of the nose. He put it in his mouth and felt the moist firm texture.

'Oh, this tastes of pickled plum.'

'That's right. I use pickled plum and *shiso*.'

Sentaro tasted the soup again in admiration. 'This is amazing...' He gave the two elderly ladies a querying look. 'How do you make this soup, and the kombu?'

He knew of course there was no easy answer to his question, but it was the only way he knew to convey his feelings. Tokue giggled.

'It's not so difficult. This is a Confectionery Group standard. We make it every New Year.'

'That's right. Toku was sick this year so I managed to do the soup by myself, but I had to use bought kombu. Today Toku stirred herself into action at last to make her pickle in time for your visit.'

'Thank you very much,' Sentaro said. He looked at his bowl and noticed that it was nearly empty. 'I've never had sweet soup like this before.'

'Oh, isn't that lovely, Toku? He seems to like it.'

'I didn't know that sweetness could be this mild... and the flavour of kombu just seems to expand in the mouth.'

'We put a bit of salt directly in the soup, too, you know. But only a pinch because of the kombu, so you can't really tell,' Tokue said, and at last took a mouthful herself. She looked into the distance while assessing it, then her gaunt cheeks relaxed into a smile. 'Mm, the balance is just right.'

Sentaro and Miss Moriyama both nodded vigorously in agreement.

'Boss.'

'Yes.'

Tokue put the bowl down and looked Sentaro straight in the eye. 'I would say that my bean paste is just the tiniest bit on the salty side.'

'Yes, I can tell that,' he said.

'On the other hand,' she continued, 'that bean paste you were using at the shop. It had absolutely no...'

'That Chinese paste...No it didn't,' Sentaro agreed.

'That's why I thought it was sticky and the sweetness had no pep in it.'

Tokue was right. It was a question of taste, but Sentaro had always tired of that bean paste – which was of course non-salted – after a mouthful or two.

'I have the feeling that men like you who like to drink prefer bean paste with a little bit of salt in it.'

'Oh, so that's why I can eat it.'

'You don't have much of a sweet tooth but you still

148

like my bean paste, which means that the salt is probably helping.'

'No, it's the way you handle the beans – it's extraordinary.'

'But if there was no salt at all, you probably wouldn't like it as much.'

'Maybe...'

'Everyone here is the same,' Miss Moriyama said, looking round her. 'When we serve bean paste to men, they always like it better with a bit of salt.'

'Boss, which do you think is saltier? My usual bean paste or the soup you had today?' Tokue continued.

'Err...' Sentaro was baffled for a moment, not understanding exactly what he was being asked. Then his eyes lighted on the plate of salty kombu.

'The soup, maybe. Because we ate it with salty kombu.'

'Yes, it's a big difference. That's why you could eat a whole bowlful.'

'Because I like a drink?'

'It's not too much of an ordeal for you to eat bean paste with a salty flavour.'

'No, it's not.'

'But when you make bean paste you don't put a lot of salt in it, do you?'

'No. Because if I did it'd all be ruined.'

'If that's so, what about this soup? Salty kombu has a high salt content.'

'Well...um...What are you saying?'

Tokue's gaunt face was lit by the smile in her eyes. Miss Moriyama looked at her and said nothing.

'With bean paste, you don't know how much salt is used. But with the soup, it's obvious because of the salty kombu. So why don't you try using salt in another way when you make dorayaki? It could be a new type of dorayaki for people like you, who like a drink.'

Miss Moriyama clapped her hands loudly. 'Yes! There are already salted *manju* buns and salted rice cakes – it's the concept of reverse expectations.'

'So you mean, ah...salty dorayaki?'

'Yes. Sometimes it's good to go with what you like most.'

Miss Moriyama let out a long whistling breath of admiration and banged the table enthusiastically. 'She's the one! Toku was always the ideas person in the Confectionery Group.'

'Well, I just put this empty head of mine to work.'

Miss Moriyama leaned forward. 'Mr Tsujii, Toku is usually right. If she says something like this, you have to give salty dorayaki a try.'

'You think I should make salty dorayaki?'

'It'll sell,' Miss Moriyama pronounced, and Tokue mumbled in agreement.

Sentaro nodded his thanks. 'Thank you for the soup. And the new ideas. As always, I never know how to thank you enough.'

'Oh, get on with you. I was just throwing out some ideas. More importantly—' Tokue broke off and looked at Miss Moriyama, then turned her sunken eyes back to Sentaro.

Miss Moriyama gathered up the bowls and placed them on the tray. 'I'll wash these,' she said, and left.

'I'm not asking you to say any more,' Tokue said in a low voice, 'but thank you for being honest with me.'

'Uh...' Sentaro knew what she was referring to and hung his head.

'It's a shame about your mother.'

'Yes.'

'Is your father still alive and well?'

Sentaro nodded and said nothing.

'Then wouldn't it be best to go and see him?'

'It's hard to find a reason to go.'

'Really?'

'The whole mess was all my doing. It was hard especially for my mother – I did something that couldn't be undone.'

'But you paid your dues. In prison.'

'Yes.'

'Then you have to start over.'

Sentaro hung his head, unable to look Tokue in the eye. He stared at the salty kombu on the plate.

'I thought about it a long time, too...how to start over. The boss came to my rescue and I started working in that kitchen, but...' Sentaro paused, 'all I thought about was getting away from there.'

'But it's no wonder if you don't like sweet foods.'

'Yes, but...' Sentaro drew a deep breath, 'now I

want to keep the shop going. Do it my way.'

'I can see that. I can definitely see you making your own style of dorayaki. That's why—'

'What?'

'Well, to tell the truth, there's nothing more I can teach you about making bean paste. It's up to you now – just do what you want. Have confidence in yourself.' Tokue's eyes glistened. 'You can do it, Sentaro,' she said.

22

Salty dorayaki. It was easy to talk about, but not so simple when it came to actually making them. Sentaro asked his suppliers to get him well-known brands of natural sea salt such as Ako from the Seto Inland Sea or Yanbaru from the Okinawan island of Iejima. But before he could reach a point where the quality of the salt would make any difference, he had to grapple with the problem of exactly where and how to add salt to the dorayaki in order to make a new kind of confectionery – that was the part he couldn't figure out.

At first Sentaro tried increasing the amount of salt he mixed into the bean paste. Ordinarily he would add only a pinch to a four-kilogram batch – one gram at the most. He tried increasing it to two grams, then three grams. And something mysterious happened when he did; the salty flavour stood out against the sweetness, clear and fresh – an unexpected blossoming of flavour. The taste was fleeting and not overpowered by sweetness. He found it refreshing. But that was only when he added salt in minute quantities. Once he increased the amount of salt – specifically to three or more grams per four-kilogram batch – the flavour abruptly turned coarse, and lost all subtlety. It was like an over-salty soup that became inedible beyond a certain point – not a taste he could serve in dorayaki.

No matter how much he thought about how to add salt to the bean mixture, Sentaro could only come up with using the same method as he always had: to cautiously add tiny amounts as he mixed the beans. Not only was that the most he could do, it was, he felt, the only way.

What should he do then? The obvious answer was to try adding salt to the pancake, so he decided to experiment with the batter. As always, he blended equal amounts of eggs, sugar and soft flour. Then he added some baking powder to leaven, honey and sweet rice wine, and a tiny dash of green tea for flavouring. Next he divided the batter into several bowls, put varying amounts of salt in each, and cooked the pancakes.

On the day he tried this, the owner happened to drop in on her way back from the doctor's, just as he had finished the cooking. She looked over the books for the past few days. 'This is terrible,' she said, clicking her tongue in disapproval.

'I'm just in the middle of trying something new,' Sentaro told her.

The owner usually avoided eating dorayaki because of the sugar level, but her interest was piqued. 'Let's see,' she said, reaching for one.

Her reaction was immediate. 'Ugh, it's salty,' she spat.

'Because it's a salty dorayaki.'

'What is this...? It makes you thirsty.'

'I have one that's less salty.'

'There's something *poor* about it.'

Poor? Sentaro was taken aback by her choice of words. He took a bite of one and chewed on it slowly, carefully assessing the taste.

'Do you think so? I think it's actually quite good.'

Sentaro honestly thought that. It was a novel taste. He liked the experience of tasting salt when he expected sweetness – it was refreshing. But after taking a second and third bite, he began to see what the owner was getting at. Unlike the impression left by the first mouthful, now there was only an unpleasant salty aftertaste. At the same time, the rich, rounded flavour of the pancake faded. The trick was shamelessly exposed.

'I see what you mean,' Sentaro said after he finished eating it. 'You don't feel like eating another one.' He looked at her.

'It might catch people's eye. You could try selling it.' The owner spoke flatly, and to Sentaro she might as well have been saying she disapproved.

There was no changing the fact, however, that Doraharu was in a tight corner. If they didn't come up with something new there would be no future.

'As I've said many times already, we can't go on like this. Now is a good time to finish up with dorayaki.'

This statement went one step further than her usual pronouncements on the subject.

155

'I hope I feel a lot better about all this by the time that cherry tree blooms,' she said, pointing through the glass door. 'What's your opinion, Sentaro? Don't you think it'd be better to make a fresh start as an *okonomiyaki* shop? Or how about *yakitori*? You'd like it if we could serve alcohol as well, wouldn't you?'

'Nope. Like I said before, I don't think we should give up on dorayaki.'

'But the reality is you can't draw customers any more.'

It was on the tip of Sentaro's tongue to say that was because of customers' attitude towards Tokue but now—then he stopped himself and took a deep breath.

'Please, may I ask for your patience just a little longer?'

'My patience...?'

'If you've got the leeway to renovate the shop and open a new one, can't you take a final punt on dorayaki?'

'You're too much, Sentaro. I mean to say – you didn't even like dorayaki, did you? I know you're only at this shop because of your debts. Why on earth have you taken it into your head to pull your finger out now? If we sell *okonomiyaki* you could serve alcohol too – wouldn't that be more your taste? I think it'd be much better for you. Why are you being so stubborn about dorayaki now?'

'Well...I—'

'And one more thing. If we're going to renovate, it has to be now.'

'Why's that?'

'Because my savings are running out. If we miss this chance I might have to let the whole business go. Do you understand? Now that would really be a betrayal of my husband. If we don't do something while I still have the means, we'll be up to our ears and forced to fold. What would *you* do, Sentaro?' The owner paused. 'With all I have to worry about, you end up proposing...salty dorayaki?'

'Um...'

She took another bite of her partially eaten dorayaki. 'It's even saltier cold! You try it.'

At her insistence Sentaro took the piece she broke off to offer him, and put it in his mouth. She was right about the flavour changing as it cooled. The saltiness now tasted much stronger than was desirable.

'I appreciate your trying something new. But reality is reality. It's the end of January now...I have a proposal.'

'Huh?'

'I will make a decision based on sales at the end of February. If sales grow next month, like before, you can keep on with dorayaki. If not, we give up. An Osaka-style shop might be nice, with *okonomiyaki* and octopus balls...we can do both, can't we? Customers can sit at the counter and drink. Average takings per head should go up and...oh, since you've already paid back a lot of your debt, I'll let you off the rest. Whatever you can pay me by the end of February will be enough.'

'What?'

'You've almost paid it all back, you know. I'll let you off the rest. Let's do this with good grace, Sentaro. There are times in life when we have to make changes.'

Sentaro said nothing for a while. 'All right,' he said.

'Whatever happens, next month we make a new start. Got it?'

'I understand.'

The owner put her leftover dorayaki on a plate and thrust it back to him.

23

Doraharu

Dear Tokue,

How are you? The weather is still so cold and wintry, I hope you are staying warm and haven't caught any more colds.

I'm still struggling along, though I did take a hint from what you said last time and immediately started experimenting. I'm sure you can guess what I mean – salty dorayaki!

At first I tried increasing the amount of salt in the bean paste, but that was a failure. It made me realize, however, that the amount you always put in is exactly right. As it would be! So nothing has changed with the bean paste.

Then I started thinking about what else I could add to justify calling it a salty dorayaki. Too simple, maybe, but next I tried putting salt in the pancake. This produced some very interesting dorayaki. If you eat it while it's still warm the flavour is like nothing you've ever tasted before, and I thought I might have found the answer. But then after a while the saltiness becomes overpowering. Like a subtle flavouring that gets to be too much. I tried reducing the salt so that wouldn't happen, but then it becomes so subtle you don't get that surprise taste with the first bite.

So I discovered that putting salt in the pancake is difficult too, and came to the conclusion that the answer is not simply dissolving salt into the bean paste mixture or the pancake batter. I think the reason the salty kombu works in the sweet soup we ate is because it acts as an accent on the palate. If it were a salty soup, with a generous amount of salt in it already, then there would be resistance to adding any more.

So I don't know. I need to find something that will keep its own texture and flavour, like the salty kombu in sweet soup, but can bring out the taste of the dorayaki at the same time. With things as they are at Doraharu I don't have that much time to think about it, but I'm trying to practice what I learned from you about Listening, and maybe that will help. I still haven't given up hope. But sales are still not picking up. At the moment I only make a fresh batch of bean paste once every four days. When I think of how busy we were just six months ago I can hardly believe it.

Every day I try to open up my mind and listen. The reality is, though, that I don't hear anything yet.

I'd like to come and see you again sometime when the weather gets warmer. This time I'll bring Wakana with me. We can decide then about letting the canary go free.

Sorry to go on so much about all my problems. But I know it's no use trying to pretend otherwise with you, so I took the liberty of writing my thoughts.

I will keep trying and hope that perhaps one day the god of confectionery will whisper words in my ear too.

Yours sincerely,

Sentaro Tsujii

Dear Sentaro

Please excuse me if I skip the formalities. I'm sorry that my inconsiderate remarks seem to have set you off on a wild quest.

You are right, however, about salt being a very tricky ingredient to use. It doesn't matter so much in savoury food, but when you use it in sweet foods it mustn't be too noticeable. That is an iron rule. It can only be used in minute quantities, which means, as you point out, that it becomes an accent to the flavour. That certainly describes the relationship between sweet soup and salty kombu.

But you also discovered something very important, which is, I believe, the beauty of the concept. And that is, that sweet soup and salty kombu have nothing in common, but somebody thought to put them together so that people with a sweet tooth and those who do not like sweet things could both eat the soup.

Likewise, dorayaki are already perfect as they are. But if you think of them in the same way you might come up with something that would go well with them. I'll give it some thought too.

I know you may not be able to hear anything now, even if you try, but please don't give up. I feel sure that one day you will find whatever it is you seek, and that the spark that leads to it will come from hearing some kind of voice. People's lives never stay the same colour forever. There are times when the colour of life changes completely.

I'm nearly at the end of my time, and because of this there are things I know. I had to spend my whole life living with the consequences of Hansen's disease. Looking back on what life was like when

I first entered the sanatorium, then ten years later, twenty years later, thirty years later, and now I'm approaching the end, I can see how different the colour of my days were at each stage.

It was a hard life. That has to be said, and it's one way of putting it. But as life passed by while shut up in here, I came to understand something. I realized that no matter how much we lost, or however badly we were treated, the fact is we are still human. All we can do is keep on going with our lives, even if we lose limbs, because this is not a fatal illness. In the midst of darkness and a struggle we had no hope of winning, I held on to this one thing – the fact of our humanity – and I was proud of it.

That's maybe why I tried to Listen, because I believe that human beings are living creatures with this capability. When I Listened, I sometimes heard things.

I Listened to the birds that visited Tenshoen, and the insects, trees, grass and flowers. To the wind, rain and light. And to the moon. I believe they all have voices. I can easily spend a whole day Listening to them. When I am in the woods at Tenshoen the whole world is there too. When I hear stars whispering at night I feel part of the eternal flow of time.

Sentaro, things are difficult for you now because the customers aren't coming back, are they? You are too kind to say so directly, but my guess is that the bad period that started because of me is not over. The Leprosy Prevention Act doesn't exist any more but public opinion hasn't changed all that much, it seems. Don't let all that stop you from trying to open your ears to the voices all around you. Listen, and keep listening, for the voices that ordinary people can't hear, and keep making your dorayaki. I am sure that if you do, the future will open out for both you and Doraharu.

I'm sorry. Please forgive me for saying the same thing over and over. But it's what I believe. I know you can get through the difficult stage you are going through.

When it gets warmer please do come and visit again. I look forward to seeing Wakana too.

Take care,

Tokue Yoshii

24

The end of February approached, bringing with it the winds heralding spring. Gusts rolling in from the south shook the tiny buds that were beginning to appear on the cherry tree outside the shop. As temperatures rose, more and more people could be seen walking with coats tucked under their arms. Sentaro kept the window closed almost completely to prevent dust blowing into the shop, but he left a small gap through which he called out 'Freshly cooked dorayaki!'

Bit by bit, sales were picking up. Although Sentaro had not given up on the idea of salty dorayaki, and was still mulling over how best to make them, the turn of the season seemed to bring about a change of heart in former customers, who began to drift back and show their faces again. They stood outside the shop self-consciously making remarks such as 'It's been a while' or 'I suddenly felt like eating a dorayaki'. Sentaro merely responded with a smile.

There was a slight softening in the owner's face, too, as she went over the books. 'If you keep on like this we might be able to make a go of it,' she said sometimes. Sentaro was cautiously optimistic, believing that although the crisis was not yet over, he did at last have some breathing space.

Then one day, in the still of the evening after the winds had subsided, the owner appeared through the door near the counter. She was followed by a gum-chewing young man.

'This is the shop manager, Mr Tsujii,' she said to the youth, pointing her chin in the direction of Sentaro.

'Tanaka's the name,' he responded, still chewing, and with a nod of greeting that could only be described as perfunctory.

'I've been thinking things over and...' the owner paused, 'I know this is sudden, but – look here, Sentaro, I want you to work with this lad.' She looked at him. 'Come on,' she urged.

Tanaka took a step forward. He looked about twenty-two or -three, and wore his jeans low over the behind, in the current fashion.

'Work with?' Sentaro repeated, not getting her meaning.

'He's my nephew. He went to cooking school and got a job in a restaurant, but had trouble getting on with some people. You know how it is with kitchens and cooks. It can be a tough world.' Her tone rose, as if asking Sentaro to agree with her. 'So then he was in a position where he had to quit,' she continued, 'and all winter he's just been hanging around. Isn't that right?'

Tanaka gave a forced smile, and cocked his head bashfully.

'Now, Sentaro. I want you to listen to me, because I've made an executive decision as owner of this shop. Next month we're renovating. I want us to sell dorayaki *and* okonomiyaki from now on. We'll sell savoury food as well as sweet.'

'Renovate, but...?'

'Yes. I know it'll be cramped. But luckily customers are coming back, and a lot are school kids, so my nephew will be able to talk with them.'

'But, hold on a minute....' Sentaro tried to cut her short, but couldn't find the right words.

'I understand. Truly I do.' She waved her hand wildly, as if to push away his objections. 'It's sudden, I know. And I feel bad about that. But you have to realize at my stage of life I need to think seriously. Then, just by coincidence, my nephew...well I've always been fond of him since he was a little boy, and he did train to be a cook...well, you know, I started thinking about it a while ago. I want you to do me a favour. I'd like you to pull him into shape. He's still got a lot of rough edges. But he's a good kid, really.'

'But you said if sales grew we could keep on as we were...' Sentaro could barely suppress the anger and bitterness that was beginning to well up.

'If anyone can do it, you can. Look how determined you were to get sales back on track after they'd dropped so far. I finally understood what my husband

169

saw in you. That's why we'll keep the name. We'll still be Doraharu. You keep making your dorayaki. But at the same time I want you to train up the future head of this business. I'm asking you, Sentaro.'

She prodded her nephew. 'Thank you,' he mumbled with a faint smirk, and bowed.

'The *okonomiyaki* pancake grill can go here.' She pointed to the space next to the window, 'and we'll move the dorayaki griddle in the back.'

Ignoring Sentaro, she began discussing the renovations with her nephew. It was clear the space for dorayaki was not going to be in the shopfront any more.

Sentaro stood watching them, there was nothing he could say.

25

Beams of light from the streetlamps filtered through the gap between the curtain and its rail. Sentaro lay curled up on his futon, staring up at the geometrical patterns of light on the ceiling.

A cat yowled outside.

Nearly a month had passed since Sentaro had quit working at Doraharu. He had been holed up in his flat ever since, oblivious to the spring weather and only going out to get food from the convenience store. He spent the days sitting around, indifferent to the passage of time.

But it could not go on. Sentaro understood that very well, hence today he had bought a job-vacancy magazine along with his instant noodles. He planned to ring and inquire if he found anything suitable. He didn't care what kind of work, he wasn't going to be picky, and he had the stationery to write up a résumé for a job application if necessary. But after turning page after page he found nothing. His age disqualified him for every position he looked at, and the very few companies that made no mention of age were, without exception, seeking applicants with special qualifications. Sentaro had no qualification apart from an ordinary driver's license. He had nothing. The gateways to all mid-career opportunities were firmly closed to him.

Grumbling to himself, he reverted to his now usual position on the floor and lay in a heap next to a pile of unwashed clothes. Night came and still he lay there, unmoving. A cat meowed outside and he wondered idly what it looked like. It sounded as if it were calling to him. Was it meowing out of loneliness? Or in search of a mate? Why did it meow? Was it male, or female?

Sentaro expelled a shallow breath. He thought of Tokue's letter. 'Listen,' she'd written. What did she mean by that? What on earth was he supposed to hear?

He didn't have the faintest clue what the voices that he could actually hear – like the cat – were saying. How was he supposed to hear something like the whispers of adzuki beans?

Sentaro stared at the dingy wall from the corner of his eye. At the end of the day, he was a loser. He might as well face up to it; that was the only conclusion he could draw. He should just string a rope up in here and get it over with.

His eyes roamed about the room, searching for a place to attach a rope. The curtain rail was the only feasible place, he decided, but the thought of himself dangling alongside the curtain seemed ridiculous. He snorted abruptly.

'Ungrateful dog, am I?' he murmured.

Those were the words the owner had thrown at

him when he quit Doraharu. Sentaro thought so, too, and didn't argue back.

'Do you know what my husband went through to help out an ex-con like you? How can you have the face to abandon my nephew? What kind of person are you? What would your parents say?' she yelled.

The day he had asked the owner over to hand in his resignation, and the money he still owed her, she'd thrown one insult after another at him, calling him, amongst other things, a criminal who knew nothing about gratitude.

Sentaro did not say a word in his defence. He simply stood there and took it, because he knew that there was truth in what she said. There was nothing he could do about it though. He'd always let people down – everybody, including his parents.

He did not know when or why his fall had begun, but he sensed the seeds of it had always been in him, ever since he was small. It was nothing sudden. It was not failure to try and live an honest life – the result of leading an honest life was the wreckage of his days now. In short, Sentaro suffered because he was who he was.

That's why tonight once again he was struggling with himself. He groaned like an injured animal, feeling as if he would suffocate whichever way he turned. He thought again how to hang himself, but he had no rope. Maybe he could use packing string, or a belt.

By the side of his desk sat a cardboard box of cooking implements which the owner had let him

bring from Doraharu since they wouldn't be needed any more – his only compensation after years of
work there. It contained his beloved copper pot with
bowls stacked inside, the rubber spatula and *dora*
spoon, the beater, the palette knife and his cook's
outfit.

Sentaro looked over and silently took in the irreg-
ular-shaped silhouette formed by these objects poking
out of the box. He recalled his days in the shop: faces
of customers waiting in line on the other side of the
window; school kids sitting at the counter chatting
away in high spirits; the cherry tree and its changing
appearance through the seasons; Tokue, standing
beneath the cherry tree.

'Dorayaki...'

He could feel the bowl and rubber spatula in his
hands. He saw the sparkle of freshly cooked adzuki.
He smelled their rich aroma.

'Dorayaki...fresh dorayaki.'

Sentaro bit his lip.

'Dorayaki, fresh dorayaki.'

Sentaro spoke the words again and felt something
roll down his cheek. He clenched his fists, drew a deep
breath and gritted his teeth.

I know you can get through...That's what Tokue
had written. He'd let her down already. He hadn't kept
any of his promises.

'Tasty, fresh dorayaki, how about it?' His voice
trembled.

Clutching the pillow in his arms, Sentaro buried his head in it. An image of the cherry tree outside the shop rose in his mind again. No doubt it was proudly blooming again this year, stopping passers-by in their tracks with its glorious cloud of flowers. Petals would be wafting down into the shop. And the school girls who complained about petals in their dorayaki... Would they be there? Were those girls still going to the shop under its new manager?

26

That night, Sentaro had a dream.

Somewhere, in a place he does not know, he is climbing a slope amid rolling hills. Below he sees something sparkling blue. It is a broad, slow-flowing river. He stops and looks at the surface, maybe a dozen metres below. The junction of currents below the surface is as clear as if he were standing in it. Several strands of sparkling white lines floating on the surface meet up and separate in constantly shifting patterns.

What is this? Sentaro cannot fathom what he sees. Then understanding dawns: these are flower petals. His gaze follows the flow upstream where a chalk-white cloud meets his eyes. He sees that the entire riverbank sloping up to the mountains is a carpet of cherry blossom in full bloom.

Sentaro climbs step by step in the direction of this luminescence. Birds sing and the breeze carries the fragrance of flowers. Gradually he draws closer to the cloud of cherry blossoms. Sparkling petals fall around him, drifting down from the sky above.

He hastens over to the trees and walks among them. Sentaro slowly turns his head to gaze in rapture at each and every tree. Blossom surrounds him on all sides, as if he is at the centre of a deep, sparkling lake. He senses the full force of emotion that has been dormant in the trees all year, waiting for this once-a-year explosion of joy: their pure, unadulterated happiness. Sentaro turns around and around as he makes his way over to the slope's edge, where he looks down on the river. A cool breeze rises from the glistening water.

A fragrance seems to wrap around him as dancing petals borne upward on currents of rising air envelope him from the feet up. The light permeates everything, radiating from the surface of the blue water, from the proudly blooming flowers, and pouring down from the sky.

Two birds skim the water and take off into flight. Sentaro lingers, wondering where he is.

'Sentaro,' he hears a young girl's voice say, and turns around to look.

Among the rows of cherry trees he sees a teahouse, with a fluttering banner at the entrance advertising *goheimochi* grilled rice cakes. He smells a savoury aroma that whets his appetite.

'Sentaro.' It is the girl's voice again.

The voice seems to come from the direction of wooden tables outside the teahouse, where customers sit viewing the blossoms while they eat and drink. He moves closer and sees a young girl sitting at a table slightly apart from the others.

'Huh?' he exclaims.

The girl stands and bows in Sentaro's direction. He

knows immediately who she is.

'Look.' She points with a smile to the collar of her pure white blouse. 'My mother made it.'

The blouse glows in the spring sunshine. Petals flutter through the air and settle on it.

'That's nice.' Sentaro speaks to her in a respectful tone, as if addressing an adult.

'Yes,' she answers.

'So this is the place?'

'Yes, this is it. My hometown. This beautiful place.'

Sentaro sits down facing her. On the table is a plate of rice dumplings coated with sweet bean paste, along with a small pot and a teacup.

'Please,' the girl says, indicating them with her hand.

Sentaro looks at it. The teacup contains what appears to be hot water with floating petals.

'Did these petals fall in?'

She shakes her head. 'No. This is cherry-blossom tea. It's a little bit salty with a lovely smell of flowers.'

'Really? Cherry-blossom tea?' Sentaro has never heard of it before. 'Cherry-blossom tea,' he murmurs again, and at that moment feels something pierce his breast. A petal fluttering through the air penetrates his chest, becoming a momentary beam of light before it disappears. But no, it is not gone.

A little bit salty with a lovely smell of flowers...The words linger and echo inside him. Suddenly the cherry blossoms all around seem to expand and Sentaro blinks.

'What's it made from?' he says, lifting up the tea-cup to examine it closer.

'We pickle it at home,' the girl replies. 'Look inside.' She points to the pot with long, straight fingers.

Sentaro lifts the lid and sees that the liquid is filled with peach-coloured flowers. He breathes in the intense, sweet aroma.

'Ahhh...'

'It's a double-flowered variety, not your usual *somei yoshino*. We pickle it with salt,' the girl says.

'It's lovely.'

Sentaro is annoyed by his inability to say more.

'You steep it in hot water and it becomes cherry blossom tea.'

He listens and peers into the teacup again, as if to compare it with the pickled blossom. Two perfect flowers twist and turn as they rise gently to the surface. They have been picked with the sepal intact to preserve the shape.

Entranced, Sentaro watches the spiralling flowers. He smells the full, deep aroma, then raises the cup to his lips and takes a sip. The flavour opens up in his mouth like a flower. A fresh trail of salt trickles down his cheek.

A little bit salty with a lovely smell of flowers... Exactly as the girl said it would be. The saltiness and aroma interact with perfect union.

This is it.

Sentaro gently places the cup back on the table and

gazes with fascination at the pickled double-flowered cherry blossom in the pot. This is it – the thing he has been seeking.

'The saltiness is just enough so you can still appreciate the taste of the flower. I could put one or two flowers in dorayaki batter...'

Sentaro half-rises from his seat. The girl has disappeared. Her smiling face, the white blouse with the petals sticking to it – all is gone. He stands up and hastily looks around. Everything has vanished. Nothing is left of the tables, customers looking at flowers or the teahouse with its banner. All he sees are shining white cherry blossoms. The table he touched only a few moments ago, with the dumplings, teacup and pot of pickled cherry blossom, has also vanished.

Enveloped in the glare of shining white cherry blossom he calls the girl's name over and over. But the only movement is the steady drift of flowers dropping to the ground, nothing else changes. Finally Sentaro realizes this world he has strayed into is not real. He senses that he will soon return to the waking world and knows he has to find the girl. Where is she? There is something he needs to ask: where were you born and raised? He recalls she told him once there was a river, and beautiful cherry blossoms, and something about pickling the cherry blossoms.

He wants to know: did you ever eat them with sweet food?

27

On the other side of the long holly hedge the cherry blossoms were in full bloom. Falling petals spiralled to the ground on the breeze.

Sentaro and Wakana exchanged few words as they walked along, but at intervals Sentaro asked her neutral questions.

'What club will you join in school?'

'Err...I haven't decided yet.'

It was Sentaro who had contacted Wakana. He had his doubts about the propriety of a grown man phoning a 15-year-old girl to ask her to accompany him somewhere, but with the issue of Marvy to resolve they needed to go to Tenshoen together.

Ever since the dream, Sentaro had been unable to get pickled cherry blossom out of his head. When a search on the internet revealed that it actually existed, he was so deeply overcome he closed his eyes. He toyed with the idea of immediately ordering some to try, but decided against it, as he was no longer set up for cooking and experimenting with dorayaki. Besides, if those pickled cherry blossoms really did exist in that place then that was what he wanted to use, and he still did not know where it was.

He had sent Tokue a postcard saying that he and Wakana were coming to pay a visit. There was a chance it might not have been delivered yet, but he thought it unlikely she would be away from Tenshoen. He was fairly sure that if they just arrived things would work out somehow; he knew where she lived and if they did not find her at the shop they could go to her unit.

A canopy of inviting blue sky stretched across the woods at Tenshoen. Clouds of cherry blossom and gleaming chestnut leaves swayed in the breeze on the other side of the hedge.

'The new school year starts soon and you'll be moving up...It really does seem like spring now,' Sentaro said.

'Yep, spring's here.'

'The cherry trees are feeling at their best now too, I guess.'

'Prob'ly.'

Wakana wasn't being particularly communicative, so Sentaro decided to broach the topic himself.

'I wanted to talk to you about something. About the canary...'

'Marvy?'

'Yes, Marvy. Tokue wants to let him go. She says she can tell he wants to be free.'

'Um.'

'You know Tokue wasn't allowed to leave here for a long time, so I guess she understands what it feels like to be a bird in a cage. If he can fly, I think it might be better to let him go. If he has somewhere to go for food I'm sure he could survive in the woods here.'

'Yeah, maybe,' Wakana replied briefly, without even hesitating.

Sentaro was surprised at how readily she accepted the idea.

'Also, you probably already know, but Doraharu is no longer.'

Wakana was walking behind Sentaro. 'Yeah, I know.' She paused a few beats before asking, 'Why'd you quit?'

'The owner didn't think dorayaki were right for the times any more.'

'I don't have anywhere to go on the way home from school now.'

'Surely not,' Sentaro said.

'Actually...' Wakana drew closer.

'What?'

'I'm going to school part-time.'

'Really?'

'Yes. So I can work during the day.' The look in her eyes hardened for a moment.

'Oh, is that so?' Sentaro didn't know what to say. He simply forged on. 'Well, whatever happens, it's up to you to make the best of it.'

'That's what everyone says. My homeroom teacher too. But nobody else is part-time.'

'I suppose so,' Sentaro said.

'What about you? Did you go to a normal school?

Did you study hard?' she asked.

'I went to normal school, but...'

Wakana made no reply and Sentaro looked back. He saw she was trailing her hand along the prickly hedge with a frown. 'I'm the only one in my class who'll study part-time.'

'Oh...But you'll...I'm—'

'We don't have any money. That's why I have to get some work. That's why I went to Doraharu – to ask for a job. But it was gone.'

'I'm sorry.'

'Me too. Tokue said before it'd be okay to work there. That's why I was disappointed big time. And a bit mad too. Aren't you going to make dorayaki somewhere else?'

'Well, I'd like to.'

'Yeah, I thought so.'

'Wish I could open a shop with you.'

Sentaro was surprised at himself for saying such a thing, even if it was in jest. But in that moment, he felt as if he was throwing off his old self, the one who had withdrawn from the world ever since quitting Doraharu.

Wakana moved closer to Sentaro's side to show her silent agreement. With her fingertips she tapped the bag slung from her shoulder.

'I brought a present for Tokue.'

'Really, what is it?'

'Take a guess.'

Sentaro could not think of anything. He searched his mind and randomly came up with 'A winter vest.'

'Nope,' Wakana teased him. 'It's already spring. Why would I get something like that?'

'Okay, what? Give me a hint at least.'

'It's not food.'

'I don't know then.'

In the end Sentaro couldn't guess. By now they had passed the hedge and reached the National Hansen's Disease Museum. The cherry trees were in bloom here too, but the silence was pronounced, as always.

'Ahh, here we are again.' It wasn't clear whether Wakana was speaking out of nostalgia or discomfort. They passed the statue of the mother-and-daughter pilgrims outside the museum entrance, and continued on the path along the edge of the grounds.

'This blossom is amazing.'

'Isn't it? I feel like I'm in a dream.'

The avenue of trees lining the path was a magnificent sight. It seemed to Sentaro as if the trees had absorbed all surrounding light in order to shine it down on them from above. He saw other people, perhaps neighbourhood residents or former patients, out enjoying the spectacle.

'Do you know where Tokue lives?' Wakana asked.

'I've never been there. But I know the address, so if we don't find her at the shop we can check the map.'

'Hmm,' said Wakana with a doubtful nod.

As usual there were people gathered in the vicinity of the shop, passing the time of day. All were elderly. Many of the men wore sunglasses.

Sentaro peeked in through the open door. It was the time he had written on the postcard, but he didn't see Tokue anywhere. 'Looks like we'll have to find her at home,' he said.

Then Wakana gently prodded Sentaro's elbow. 'That lady over there is looking at us – we met her last time, didn't we?'

The woman whom Sentaro remembered from his last visit rose from her seat at the farthest table.

'Ah, it's Miss Moriyama.'

Sentaro and Wakana nodded in greeting to her and waited as she slowly made her way over.

'Hello. So we meet again.' Sentaro deliberately spoke in a bright tone.

'Ahh...' Miss Moriyama faltered.

'We came to see Tokue. I only just sent the postcard to say we're coming so it might not have arrived yet.'

'Ahh...' Miss Moriyama covered her misshapen lips with one hand as she attempted to get words out. Then, at a complete loss, she closed her eyes for a moment. 'Mr Tsujii. I took delivery of the postcard. Would you mind sitting down for a bit, please?'

Though gently expressed, there was no refusing her request. Sentaro and Wakana exchanged glances as they sat down in the seats Miss Moriyama indicated.

'Mr Tsujii and...' she paused, 'Wakana.'

'Yes, but that's a nickname.'

'I, ah, want to tell you something...'

'What?'

There was a moment of silence. 'Dear Toku passed away.'

Sentaro's jaw dropped. He jumped to his feet. Wakana made a startled movement.

Sentaro felt as if an invisible fist of all the unseen forces in the world – wind, time and space – had suddenly struck him in the chest. He made stuttering sounds, unable to form words.

Miss Moriyama did not take her wizened eyes away from his face. 'Toku gave me your contact address before. But I don't know where it went. So last week I went to the shop, and found it was an *okonomiyaki* shop now. I asked the young man there if he knew your phone number, but he said he had no idea. I was in quite a pickle, I didn't know what to do.'

Sentaro held his face in his hands, unable to speak. Belatedly, he bowed his head in thanks to Miss Moriyama.

It was all he could do to get the words 'I'm so sorry' past his lips.

'It was ten days ago. When she passed away.'

'It can't be true, it can't be true,' Wakana repeated pleadingly.

'I went to see her at home the day before. She looked exhausted. But she insisted it was only fever and didn't want to go to the clinic. So I stayed with her. That was when she gave me a letter, just in case. I told her if she was that bad she should ask you to come here, but she didn't like the idea. A letter would be fine, she said, whatever happened.'

Sentaro shook his head. He couldn't believe it.

'Toku thought of you like a son, you know. It was pneumonia.' She spoke bluntly, but her tone was not accusing.

Sentaro wanted to say something, but no words would come. Wakana sat rigidly next to him.

'We gave her a private send-off. It would've been nice if you were there, but your workplace had changed and it seemed you had things going on. Anyway, it was all so sudden.'

Sentaro shook his head again.

'Can I ask, err, about Tokue's—' His lips shook as he tried to get it out. 'Tokue's—' he tried again, but broke down.

Miss Moriyama pressed her fingers to the corners of her eyes. Then she answered the question Sentaro had been trying to ask. 'She's...she was laid to rest in the charnel house. With her husband.'

'Oh, I see,' he managed to mutter, but then could not hold back any longer. He put his elbows on the table and covered his face as the tears trickled out. Wakana sat beside him, looking down and swallowing convulsively.

'It's good you came, though. It just shows that

Toku's thoughts reached you. Yes, it's good...Why don't you come and see where she lived? Would that be all right?'

Sentaro nodded silently.

'Yes,' Wakana said hoarsely.

28

Miss Moriyama led Sentaro and Wakana back along the road with rows of houses, turned a corner and stopped at the entrance to a grassy courtyard. It wasn't that far from the shop. A nameplate on the side of the row building read 'Green Wind'. They followed behind Miss Moriyama, walking on stepping-stones across the garden, past three identical units to the fourth one at the far end.

She opened an unlocked sliding window door. 'You don't mind going through the back, do you?' she asked. 'That's what we always did.'

The timber frame around the entrance was worn down and white with use. They could see through the glass into a room with blue carpet flooring. A familiar birdcage was on the floor next to the window, but there was no Marvy inside. Sentaro darted a furtive glance at Wakana when he noticed. She was staring at the empty birdcage with tear-filled eyes.

'Come in, please.'

It was a small six-mat room, roughly ten square metres in total. A sink and refrigerator could be seen in what was presumably the kitchen at the back. The wooden-plank ceiling looked as though it had been made from scrap wood. Yellowed plasterboard walls were stained dark in places. The only visible furniture was a chest of drawers, a writing desk, a chipboard box used for stowing books, and a small television. Bedding and other belongings were probably stored out of sight in the wall closet.

'Is this where Tokue...in here?'

'No. She passed away in the clinic ward. But it was so sudden. I really didn't expect it.'

At Miss Moriyama's urging, Sentaro and Wakana removed their shoes, leaving them in the garden, and stepped up into Tokue's room. The kitchen area looked dim but it was sunny near the window.

There were several photographs on top of the chipboard box.

'This is Toku with her husband, Yoshiaki,' Miss Moriyama said, and brought her face up close to the photograph while she fumbled with her crippled fingers to pick up a stick of incense as an offering.

'Tokue was so pretty.' Wakana's voice was thick, as if she had a stuffy nose.

It's true, thought Sentaro.

The photographs were all black-and-white, probably taken when Tokue was in her twenties. The old-fashioned hairstyles gave them the appearance of scenes from an old film. Tokue looked vibrant, and not at all as if she were suffering from illness. With her shapely nose and eyes full of life, she resembled the young girl Sentaro had seen in his dream. She was casting a tender smile at the man standing by her side and he was clearly showing his adoration of this radiant young woman.

The photographs were confirmation of what Sentaro had heard from Tokue: her husband was a great deal older. The nape of his neck and the slope of his shoulders suggested a delicate, weakly constitution, which only confirmed what Tokue had told Sentaro. There was just one thing, however, that did not match with what she had told him. According to Tokue, her husband was tall, like a palm tree, so Sentaro had pictured a tall man, but the man in the photograph was of average height, and only slightly taller than Tokue.

This observation was no more than a momentary distraction as Sentaro's thoughts soon took another direction. Tokue looked so alive in the photograph, he choked up again when he thought of the ordeal that overshadowed the lives of this smiling couple.

Sentaro and Wakana lit sticks of incense to place in front of the photos and put their hands together in prayer.

'If it's all right with you, there're a few things I know Toku would be glad for you to have.' Miss Moriyama indicated a wooden box next to a small oven in the corner of the kitchen. It was crammed with utensils for making confectionery.

'We thought about dividing these up amongst ourselves to remember Toku by, but we're all getting on as well, and it's quite possible we could take something then keel over the next day.' Miss Moriyama smiled thinly at them.

'That's why it's better for someone like you to have them, Mr Tsujii. Everything in this room will be disposed of at the end of the month. It'll all disappear.'

Sentaro knelt next to the wooden box and stretched his hand out to touch the cooking utensils Tokue had used in the Confectionery Group. There was a copper pot and a wooden spatula for making sweet bean paste, along with a silk mesh strainer for turning bean paste from coarse into smooth. There were attachments for branding patterns on *rikkyu manju*, the sweet bean paste buns served with green tea, a mould for making *yokan* adzuki bean jelly, and a steamer for making *dango*, sweet rice ball dumplings. There were also many utensils for Western-style confectioneries: bowls in various sizes, tart trays, pound-cake tins, a palette knife, and a beater. Inside a plastic bag was a collection of metal tips for a cream-piping bag.

Sentaro recalled what Tokue had said about making sweet bean paste when she first came to Doraharu.

I've been making it for fifty years.

He remembered it clearly, along with the fleeting glimpse of pride in her face when she spoke.

He touched the utensils lightly with his fingertips. 'These have seen a lot of use.'

He held the aged wooden spatula out to Miss

Moriyama. 'I really think it's better for them to go to the Confectionery Group.'

She shook her head. 'The Confectionery Group hasn't been active for the last ten years or more.'

'What? But I thought...'

'Once we were allowed to leave here, we could buy whatever we wanted. If we want cake we can buy it at the supermarket. There wasn't the need any more for everyone to get together to make cakes.'

Sentaro nodded dumbly.

'Toku always took an active lead, so I think she was sad when things got like that.'

'She wanted to keep cooking, I suppose. Sweet things,' Sentaro said.

'Yes. Oh, there's also—' Miss Moriyama broke off and clamped her mouth shut.

Sentaro lined up all the items on the floor. Then he picked out several and wrapped them up in a cotton towel lying in the kitchen.

'Thank you. I'd be grateful for these.'

When would he ever stand in front of a griddle again? He couldn't be certain that day would come. Nevertheless, he would keep these cooking utensils to remember Tokue by.

When Sentaro had finished and sat down in the main room once again, he saw Miss Moriyama had placed a biscuit tin on the table.

'This is it.' She opened the lid to reveal a bundle

of writing paper. 'She gave me this letter before she was taken to the clinic ward. There was something she wanted to apologize to you about, and if she didn't come back I was to pass this on.' Miss Moriyama held the exposed notepaper out to Sentaro. He exchanged glances with Wakana. 'It's not finished. That's what she said.'

Sentaro took the letter from her.

'If it's all right with you, why don't you read it here, where she wrote it? It took her quite a while to get it all down. You know how slow she was at writing.'

Sentaro nodded, and opened up the letter. Once again he saw that familiar wavy handwriting, each stroke of each character painstakingly drawn.

Dear Sentaro,

Please excuse me if I skip formalities. By the time you read this, the cold weather should be letting up. I thought about not writing this letter in case I come across as an old woman repeating the same thing over and over, like a broken record, but this cold is getting worse and I worry whether I'll ever get to see you and Wakana again. So I decided to write because I want to apologize, and there's something else I simply must tell you.

First, I must apologize for letting Marvy go quite early on, even though I promised to look after him. The more I listened to his chirping, the more I realized he was asking to be let out. I hesitated when I thought about Wakana, but having suffered myself from not being free to go outside, I felt there was no reason to keep a living creature with wings locked inside a cage.

Maybe Marvy won't survive once he's away from human protection, but when I saw him staring up at the blue sky and singing, 'Let me out, let me out,' I couldn't stand it any more, and decided to set him free. Please tell Wakana I said sorry and pass on my apologies.

When I was little I didn't have any special dream about what I wanted to do when I grew up. It was wartime, and we were all more preoccupied by a vague kind of anxiety about simply staying alive. But after I became ill and realized that I would never be able to go out into society again, I started dreaming about what I wanted to be, which was hard.

As I told you before, I wanted to be a schoolteacher. I like children, and I liked learning. I studied at the school here in Tenshoen, and when I grew up I taught lessons, after a fashion, to the children who were patients here.

But if I'm really honest, all I ever wanted was to go outside that fence. I wanted to go out into society and work at an ordinary job. I wanted that for the same reasons everyone does – to be a useful member of society and make the world a better place.

I never lost that hope. It might have been a different story if I was always ill, but even after I recovered I couldn't leave the sanatorium. Though I wanted so much to work in the outside world, the reality was that I was caged in by that hedge and living off taxpayers' money.

I can't tell you how many times I wished I were dead. Deep down, I believed that a life has no value if a person is not a useful member of society. I was convinced that humans are born in order to be of service to the world and to others.

But there came a time when that changed, because I changed.

I remember it clearly. It was a night of the full moon, and I was walking alone in the woods. By then I had already begun Listening to the whispers of trees, and to the voices of insects and birds. On this night, the moon cast its pale, brilliant light on everything around me, and energy seemed to radiate from trees swaying in the wind. While I was alone on that path in the woods, I came face-to-face with the moon. And oh, what a beautiful moon it was! I was enchanted. It made me forget everything I had suffered because of this illness, about being shut up in here and never going out. Then next thing, I thought I heard a voice that sounded very much like the moon whispering to me. It said:

I wanted you to see me.
That's why I shine like this.

From then on I began to see everything differently. If I were not here, this full moon would not be here. Neither would the trees. Or the wind. If my view of the world disappears, then everything that I see disappears too. It's as simple as that.

And then I thought, what if this didn't apply to just me, what if there were no other human beings in this world? What about all the different forms of life that have the ability to be aware of the presence of others – what would happen if none of them existed either?

The answer is that this world in all its infinity would disappear.

You might think I'm deluded, but this idea changed me. I began to understand that we were born in order to see and listen to the world. And that's all this world wants of us. It doesn't matter that I was never a teacher or a member of the workforce, my life had meaning.

I was cured at an early stage of the illness and my side effects weren't bad enough to make it difficult to go outside. You gave me the opportunity to work at Doraharu. I feel truly blessed to have had that experience.

But what about a child whose life is over before he or she even turns two years old? People may wonder, in their sorrow, what point there is in a child like that even being born.

I have learned the answer to this. I am sure it is for that child to perceive wind, sky, and voices in his or her own unique way. The world that child senses exists because of it, and therefore that child's life, too, has purpose and meaning.

By the same token, my husband spent a great deal of his life fighting illness, and it may have looked as if he had much to be bitter about when he had to depart. But his life too had meaning, because he also sensed the sky and wind.

I'm sure there comes a time for everyone, not just those with Hansen's disease, when they wonder what the point of life is.

In answer, I can say that I know with certainty that life does have meaning.

Of course, knowing that doesn't mean that all our problems are suddenly solved, and sometimes simply getting on with life feels like a never-ending ordeal.

But I was very happy, you know. I was happy when we won the court case, and the law that kept us confined was abolished. At last I was able to go out into the world and walk about freely. We fought decades for that.

But with joy also came pain. We were free to go beyond the hedge and walk the streets if we wanted. We could ride buses and trains. We could also travel. Naturally that was a source of great happiness, and I will never forget what it was like to go outside for the first time after fifty long years of being shut up in here. Everything looked so shining and bright. But I started to notice something while I was walking around outside – wherever I went, I knew nobody and had no family. I always felt lost and alone in a strange country.

It was too late. By the time I was told that I could go out into society for the first time in decades and start over, it was much too difficult. If I had become free twenty years

201

earlier I might have managed to start a new life outside. There were many of us like that, in our sixties and seventies, for whom it was too late.

We discovered that once we experienced the joy of being out in the world and free again, the greater the happiness, the more we felt the pain of lost time and lives that could never be returned. Perhaps you understand that feeling. When any of us went outside we always came back exhausted. Not just physical exhaustion, but a deeper exhaustion that comes from bearing a pain that will never go away.

That's why I made confectionery. I made sweet things for all those who lived with the sadness of loss. And that's how I was able to live out my life.

Sentaro, your life is meaningful too.

The time you suffered behind bars, your finding dorayaki – I believe it all has purpose. All experience adds up to a life lived as only you could. I feel sure the day will come when you can say: this is my life.

You may never become a writer or a master dorayaki cook, but I do believe there will be a time when you can stand tall as yourself in your own unique way.

The first time I ever saw you I was taking my regular weekly outing. I was walking along that street enchanted by the cherry blossoms, when I smelt something sweet on the wind and found Doraharu. Then I saw you. I saw your face.

Your eyes were so sad. You had a look that made me want to ask what it was that made you suffer so. It was how my eyes used to appear, when I was resigned to being fenced in by that prickly hedge for the rest of my life. That's what drew me to stand outside your shop.

Then I had a thought. If my husband had not been forcibly sterilized, and I could have had a child, that child would be about the same age as you. After that

In the latter part of the letter the writing grew larger and the shape of the characters began to disintegrate. And then it broke off, unfinished. Sentaro closed his eyes with the letter still in his hands. For some time, nobody

203

spoke. Wakana, who had been watching Sentaro as he read the letter, eventually broke the silence.

'I wish I'd come sooner.'

Sentaro opened his eyes and looked at her. She took the bag from her shoulder, pulled out a paper bag with a red bow attached, and gently placed it in front of Tokue's photographs.

'Why don't you open it up so Toku can see?' Miss Moriyama suggested.

Wakana nodded and opened up the package with trembling fingers. It was a white blouse.

'I can't sew, so it's bought. It not expensive but...' She began to sob loudly and Miss Moriyama moved over beside her.

'I'm sure Toku is very happy right now.' She picked up the blouse, spread out the sleeves and held it up in front of the photograph. 'Isn't this lovely, Toku. Wakana brought back the blouse your mother made for you.'

Gently she ran her bent fingers across Wakana's heaving shoulders, stroking them. 'Wakana, dear.'

'Wakana,' Sentaro said, his voice choked with tears, 'thank you.'

The three sat there without speaking, waiting for their breathing to become even again.

Sentaro looked out at the garden. Time had passed quickly while they poured out their grief. The sun's rays were now infused with a deep red radiance that played over the grass. Sentaro wiped his eyes with his fingers and looked at the empty birdcage.

Miss Moriyama followed his gaze. 'Toku wondered how she was going to apologize.'

'Ah, you mean the canary?' asked Wakana.

'Yes.' Miss Moriyama shuffled over to Sentaro on her knees.

'I don't know if I should say this, seeing as how you just gave her the blouse and all, but...what do you call it? Maa—?'

'His name is Marvy.' Wakana looked up.

'She decided by herself to set Marvy free. Before she'd even asked you. She didn't know how she was going to explain it.'

'She wrote about it in the letter,' Sentaro said.

Wakana nodded. 'It's okay. I'm sure Marvy wanted to fly.'

'At first Marvy stayed around the garden and the roof just out there. He'd fly back here to eat.'

'He did?' Wakana stretched her neck to look. Her cheeks were still wet with tears. 'Flying wasn't his strong point.'

Miss Moriyama tipped her head to one side. 'Oh, not at all. I still see him here and there on different roofs.'

'He's flying? Marvy?'

'Everyone feeds him quite a bit.'

'Really?' Wakana's face relaxed for the first time since they'd entered the room.

'Isn't that great?' Sentaro said.

Wakana nodded emphatically. 'Maybe I was too protective.'

Miss Moriyama laughed suddenly. 'It may not be proper to say this about someone who's just died – someone I was fond of, moreover – but as a close friend of Toku's I feel I can say anything.'

'Like what?' Sentaro asked.

'Well, she was so overdramatic about everything.'

Sentaro and Wakana looked baffled.

'When she gave me that letter,' Miss Moriyama glanced at it sitting next to the blouse, 'I didn't mean to read it, but it wasn't in an envelope or anything, and I could see a bit of the writing. All the different forms of life that have the ability to be aware and so on. That's what she wrote about, isn't it?'

'Yes.'

'Ah, she's at it again, I thought when I saw that. Did she use the word "Listen" a lot?'

Sentaro nodded.

'Don't think badly of me, please. When Toku met someone she liked that's what she'd do. Tell them to listen to the voice of the adzuki beans, etcetera, etcetera. And how the moon whispered to her and so on.'

'But, I...' Sentaro interrupted, 'I'm grateful for that letter. So much so I want Wakana to read it later, too. It might be overdramatic but it helps me, a lot.'

Wakana pressed her eyes again. Still smiling, Miss

Moriyama looked at them. 'Shall we go for a little walk?' she said, and stood up. 'We can have a chat with Toku.'

'With Tokue?' Wakana's eyes widened.

29

Evening spread out against the sky. The changing light tinted everything it touched with the colours of sunset as a deep red unfolded across the clear blue firmament. They walked toward the charnel house, which, bathed in the full glare of the sun's rays, shone like a beacon.

'Toku asked me to join the Confectionery Group after I attempted suicide.' Miss Moriyama held out her left arm to show them. 'I cut my wrist, but didn't do a proper job of it, so I survived. I was in awful, constant pain ever since getting sick. My fingers went crooked, I got holes in my hands, and my head swelled up and never went back to normal. I got nodules on my face and head that festered with pus. For a woman, it was...I just got fed up with it all and cut my wrist.'

She turned side-on to face Wakana and Sentaro as they headed toward the charnel house.

'The pain also gets to you. That was another thing. It goes on and on, and some people choose to die. I thought I'd reached my limit. But for some reason I survived. And then Toku said to me, let's make confectionery. We'll keep going together, she said. At the time I was going out of my mind, because I couldn't even die inside this place, let alone keep living in it. Maybe she liked me. And then all that business started. Listen, open your ears – it was her pet saying. All that talk about trying to imagine the wind and the sky, what the adzuki beans saw on their travels.'

'Me too...But she made such wonderful sweet bean paste, I really believe she was telling the truth,' reflected Sentaro.

'Well, maybe, that's all well and good...' Miss Moriyama paused a few beats. 'I did as she said, and tried to listen. I put my ears up close to the adzuki beans, and I had every intention of trying my best. But you know, I didn't hear a thing. No bean-talk. What about you, Mr Tsujii? Did you ever hear the beans' voices?'

Sentaro kept walking in silence a few moments. 'No,' he said, shaking his head. 'But I think she meant we should approach the beans as if we could hear their voices.'

'That's it. That's exactly right, but she kept on about it so much I got a bit tired of it. Some people started saying she was a liar. There was a time when she was completely isolated in the Confectionery Group.'

This was news to Sentaro. 'I didn't know she went through something like that.'

'I talked with her about it at the time, when we stayed up one night. I asked her what she meant by saying all that stuff. I told her everyone was in quite a state.'

'And what did she say?'

'I don't want to disappoint you, but Toku herself said at the time that she couldn't actually hear the voices of beans. But if you live in the belief that they *can* be heard, then someday you might be able to hear them. She said that was the only way for us to live, to be like the poets. That's what she said. If all you ever see is reality, you just want to die. The only way to get over barriers, she said, is to live in the spirit of already being over them.'

'That's exactly the kind of person Tokue was. I felt like she'd already crossed the barrier.'

'What barrier?' Wakana asked.

Sentaro saw an image of the young girl who'd showed him the salt-pickled flower petals beneath the cherry blossoms. He wanted to put that into words, but held his tongue. Now was not the time to mention it. He kept his thoughts to himself.

They arrived at the charnel house. Miss Moriyama put her hands together in front of the stone cairn, shining in the evening sun, and Sentaro and Wakana also joined her in offering a prayer for the dead. But as soon as she dropped her hands she immediately set off again along the path leading into the woods.

Sentaro looked up, puzzled. Wakana also looked at her in bewilderment. 'Miss Moriyama, is that the way?'

'Yes, come on.'

'But...aren't Tokue's remains here in the charnel house?'

Miss Moriyama's answer was to beckon them on,

so they followed. The path was lined on both sides with trees that blocked the light, making it much darker than the way they had just come. A red glow still lit the sky, but night was already falling here.

Miss Moriyama began to speak again. 'I loved the way Toku talked. She used to say it was fine to think what you want about things. Hearing that from her made me feel like I could go anywhere I wanted, when all I was doing was walking along this path. But Toku was never ever a liar.'

'No, of course she wasn't,' Sentaro agreed.

'That's right. She wasn't a liar.'

Miss Moriyama stopped and turned to look at Sentaro and Wakana. It was even darker here, amongst the thick shrubs, and chestnut and pine woods. The sky visible through gaps in the trees was bright vermilion red.

'About a week before she died, one night we were having cocoa in my room and Toku started talking. She told me she'd had a strange experience.'

Wakana moved closer to Sentaro's side.

'It's all right, dear, it's nothing spooky. She told me how she'd been walking on this very path, about this time of night, when she heard voices for the first time.'

'What kind of voices?'

'Voices of the trees, she said.'

'I see,' said Sentaro simply, not knowing how to respond.

Wakana stayed close to Sentaro's side.

'She'd been telling other people to listen to the voices of the beans all that time, but in truth that was actually the first time she'd heard voices herself. Voices other than humans, that is.'

'What did they say?' Wakana sounded husky.

'Well, Toku laughed when she told me this, but what she heard was, "Good job, you did well."'

'The trees said that?'

'Yes. Toku said that whenever she walked here the trees all spoke to her, saying "Good job" or "You did it". She'd never heard that before. I can't forget her face when she told me. I've known her since she was young, and I was at her wedding too. But I'd never seen her look so happy as she did that night. I felt I should tell you both about this, because you knew her, too. I mean, she didn't need sympathy or anything. She wasn't unhappy at the end. I really do think that the trees were whispering to her. You did it, Tokue Yoshii. Good job. I believe they really said that. I mean...'

Miss Moriyama stretched her hands out to indicate the area all around them. 'This is where we plant a tree whenever one of us dies. One by one the trees have grown in number.'

Wakana stuck close to Sentaro's back. Sentaro looked at the trees all around them. Each one was a testament to a person who had spent a lifetime in here.

'It's already dark, but Toku's tree is over there.' She pointed to a nearby mound of earth with a sapling planted in the centre. 'We all talked about it and

212

decided to plant a *somei yoshino*. Because Toku loved cherry trees. She grew up near a place called Shinshiro in Aichi Prefecture. Apparently, the cherry trees there were quite something. She always used to say she wished she could see them one more time. That beech behind Toku's tree was planted for her husband when he died.'

Sentaro and Wakana stood close, gazing in silence at the trees all around them. The forest murmured with every ripple of wind that rustled its branches and leaves. As if Tokue was somewhere close nearby, telling them to open their ears and listen.

Sentaro took a step closer to the sapling. He gently trailed his hand over the young, new life. 'Tokue,' he said, stroking the branches with his fingertips.

'Oh!' Miss Moriyama gasped behind him, and Sentaro turned to look.

He saw a brilliant full moon, rising up from behind the silhouette of the holly hedge on the other side of the coppice, as if being born in that moment and place.

'Oh!' Wakana exclaimed in wonder.

The moon rose higher, hidden at intervals by trees swaying in the wind, and poured its pulsing beams of light down on them.

Sentaro turned to the cherry sapling and whispered, 'The moon has arrived.'

Author's Note

Twenty years ago I was a vocalist in a rock band and a late-night radio personality. Young people from all over Japan phoned in to tell me their grievances, sorrows, hopes and dreams, and in return I often asked my listeners: 'What is life all about?'

I wasn't asking for an answer; I simply wanted them to think about it. Their replies, however, were always much the same: I was born to be a useful member of society. If I can't be that, life has no meaning.

This admirable sentiment is much approved of in Japan, but I could never bring myself to give it the nod. I knew a child, the band-producer's son, who had died at the age of two. And I had heard about the former Hansen's patients who, by law, had been shut up in sanatoriums and isolated from society for decades, long after being cured. When that unjust legislation was repealed in 1996 their story became widely known to the public.

Some lives are all too brief, while others are a continual struggle. I couldn't help thinking that it was a brutal assessment of people's lives to employ usefulness to society as a yardstick by which to measure their value.

There has to be a reason for being born, irrespective of individual circumstance. I was thinking about this one evening, as I gazed at the thin scattering of stars in the Tokyo night sky, when I came to a decision. I would write about the meaning of life with a fresh perspective, in the context of Hansen's disease. But I was neither a patient nor a medical professional, and much time was to pass before I could begin writing. I met former patients and began to spend time with them in the sanatorium on which Tenshoen is based, and where they still live. Only then could I finally assemble the thoughts on which to base my story.

I began with the concept of a greater force that created human beings, rather than examining human society per se; the idea that we have been nurtured by the universe to prove its existence. If there is no single conscious mind capable of doing this, the existence of the universe itself becomes unverifiable. It cannot exist. Over the aeons the universe has nurtured life forms whose very awareness makes them involved in its continued existence. Hence we are all alike in having materialized on this Earth because that was what the universe so desired. The ill, the bed-ridden, and children whose lives are over before they've barely begun; all are equal in their relationship to the universe. Anyone is capable of making a positive contribution to the world through simple observation, irrespective of circumstance.

This is the idea that Tokue expresses when she writes in her letter, 'We were born in order to see and listen to the world.' It's a powerful notion, with the potential to subtly reshape our view of everything.

Durian Sukegawa

Durian Sukegawa studied oriental philosophy at Waseda University, before going on to work as a reporter in Berlin and Cambodia in the early 1990s. He has written a number of books and essays, TV programmes and films. He lives in Tokyo.

Alison Watts is a freelance translator, translating literature from Japanese into English. She lives in Ibaraki, Japan.

Also available from Oneworld

Fever Dream by Samanta Schweblin (Argentinian)

Frankenstein in Baghdad by Ahmed Saadawi (Iraqi)

Morning Sea by Margaret Mazzantini (Italian)

The Woman at 1000 Degrees by Hallgrímur Helgason (Icelandic)

The Baghdad Clock by Shahad Al Rawi (Iraqi)

The Boy Who Belonged to the Sea by Denis Thériault (Quebecois)

The Hen Who Dreamed She Could Fly by Sun-mi Hwang (Korean)

The Invisible Life of Euridice Gusmao by Martha Batalha (Brazilian)

The Peculiar Life of a Lonely Postman by Denis Thériault (Quebecois)

The Postman's Fiancée by Denis Thériault (Quebecois)

The Temptation to be Happy by Lorenzo Marone (Italian)

The Tiger and the Acrobat by Susanna Tamaro (Italian)

Things that Fall from the Sky by Selja Ahava (Finnish)

Three Apples Fell from the Sky by Narine Abgaryan (Armenian)

Umami by Laia Jufresa (Mexican)

Voices of the Lost by Hoda Barakat (Lebanese)

Zuleikha by Guzel Yakhina (Russian)